TEACHERS OF THE YEAR AGREE!

SALTWATER TAFFY

SALTWATER TAFFY

WRITTEN BY

ERIC DELABARRE

ILLUSTRATIONS BY

R. C. NASON

SEVEN PUBLISHING

Seven Publishing
P.O. Box 1123, Santa Monica, CA 90406-1123
Web site: www.SaltwaterTaffyBook.com
E-mail: seven@sevenpublishing.com

First **Seven Publishing** Hardcover Edition January 2011

ISBN 13: 978-0-9723578-0-7
LCCN: 2010902956

10 9 8 7 6 5 4 3 2 1

Manufactured in the United States of America

For more information about special discounts for bulk and educational
orders, please contact Seven Publishing at seven@sevenpublishing.com

Illustrations by R. C. Nason
Interior Design & Typesetting by Jill Ronsley
Cover Art by R. C. Nason
Cover Design by R. C. Nason & Jill Ronsley
Logo Design by Garret S. DelaBarre
Edited by Jill Ronsley
Printing & Binding by Lake Book Manufacturing

This novel is a work of fiction. All of the characters, organizations,
and events portrayed in this novel are either products of the
author's imagination or are used fictitiously.

Publisher's Cataloging-in-Publication data

DeLaBarre, Eric.
    Saltwater taffy / Eric DelaBarre ; Illustrations by R.C. Nason.
    p. cm.
    Summary: Five friends uncover a treasure map belonging to the ruthless
pirate, Jean Lafitte. The discovery thrusts them from one treasure hunting
adventure to the next.
    ISBN 978-0-9723578-0-7
    [1. Treasure troves—Fiction. 2. Pirates—Fiction. 3. Port Townsend (Wash.)—
Fiction. 4. Adventure fiction.] I. Nason, Robyn.C. II. Title.

PZ7.D36949 Sal 2011
[Fic]—dc22   2010902956

DEDICATED TO

THE TEACHERS

OF THE WORLD

CONTENTS

1

THE DEATH OF
THE GREAT PIRATE

The soles of his boots slapped against the wet cobblestone streets of Jackson Square. In the distance behind him, a steamboat chugged up the Mississippi River carrying goods to the north. It was 1823, and tonight, history would be written.

Though he walked with a limp, his pace quickened. Knowing the words resting in his mouth would cause a stir among the other pirates, he pushed forward, his long coat dancing in the wind behind him.

Entering a dead-end alley, the pirate stopped in front of a large wooden door. The sign creaked back and forth in the wind. It read, "Lafitte's Blacksmith Shop." Reaching out his scarred and weatherworn hand, he rapped on the door three times before concluding the secret knock with a kick of his leather boot. When the door opened, the massive pirate thundered forward and bellowed through his long, graying beard.

"The scoundrel is dead!" Gray Beard shouted. "Your Jean Lafitte is no more. Join me, and together we will rule these waters!"

Muffled reactions quickly shot through the candlelit room. Filled with the toughest of men, Lafitte's Blacksmith Shop was a notorious hideout for pirates. It was a place where a man's weakness was shot down faster than rum flowed from the aging barrels.

"Round of drinks for them all!" Gray Beard shouted as he stumbled forward to celebrate. "Move your bones, Barkeep. These men are thirsty for buried treasurrrrre!"

The bartender did not move. He stood frozen upon hearing the news. Surely this was just another rumor in a long line of rumors about the great pirate, Jean Lafitte.

Following the eyes in the room, which were now focused on a dark corner of the blacksmith shop, Gray Beard saw the silhouette of an ordinary-sized man shuffling in the darkness.

"Who goes there?" Gray Beard demanded.

The man pushed aside the wooden goblet before him and leaned towards the flickering candlelight. As shadows danced across his face, the jagged scar that crisscrossed his left cheek darkened. The young pirate inhaled slowly before he finally spoke.

"What say you, old man?" he grumbled. "These lies you speak shall be the death of you."

Gray Beard's eyes narrowed and the muscles in his jaw tightened like a vice. "Nary a man shall challenge me," he growled. "Show yourself and be warrrrrned."

The mysterious man rose from his chair and stepped from the shadows. Gray Beard blinked a few times to clear his vision. *Who is this man questioning me?* he wondered. When the man finally came into view, Gray Beard recognized him to be Jean Pierre Lafitte, the illegitimate son of the great pirate. Laughter leapt from Gray Beard's large belly before he leaned into his reply. "You are but a boy, Lafitte. You are no match for the likes of meeeeeee."

With eyes dark as cannonballs, Jean Pierre slowly placed his hand on the jeweled saber strapped to his hip. Some pirates shuffled in their seats while others made way. Even though Gray Beard was the size of a grizzly bear, Lafitte stalked towards him.

Silence hung in the air as the young man approached, his footsteps sifting through the sawdust on the floor. Gray Beard paused because Jean Pierre's confidence had caught him by surprise. Unaware that his feet were now in retreat, Gray Beard suddenly felt his back press against the stone wall. His heart began to race. Jean Pierre drew closer, his hand still resting on the jeweled saber. Then, slowly, oddly, Jean Pierre removed his gaze from Gray Beard's and began to exit without so much as a whisper.

"Like his father before him, a coward to the end!" Gray Beard shouted to the other pirates in the room. Without warning, Jean Pierre drew his saber, spun to his right and plunged the cold, hard metal into Gray Beard's massive belly.

"Make no mistake, sir," he said, staring at the pirate's bulging eyes. "I am Jean Pierre, and *I am ... but a boy!*" Gray

Beard's body dropped to the floor. Dark red blood slowly leaked from his body, and mixed into the sawdust beneath him. Gray Beard, the pirate, was dead.

Exiting into the balmy night air of New Orleans, Jean Pierre rested in the wind as it pushed him aimlessly through Jackson Square. He felt numb and lost track of time.

The news of his father's death produced a feeling he could not put his finger on. Was it anger towards those who had killed him? Was it guilt because he had given up trying to know his father? His questions went unanswered, but something unusual was happening. Jean Pierre felt energized. For the first time in his young life, he was hopeful and filled with purpose. Yes … Jean Pierre Lafitte was dreaming about buried treasure.

2

BARATARIA BAY

Legend had it that after his gang of pirates had overtaken a helpless cargo ship, Jean Lafitte, who demanded the lion's share of the booty, would sail alone into the swampy waters of Barataria Bay, Louisiana, to bury his treasure. Paranoid to the end, Lafitte never told anyone the location of his buried treasure—not even his son, Jean Pierre.

After his father's death, Jean Pierre sailed the waters of Barataria Bay, searching for the treasure, but he never found even a single Piece of Eight.

In 1832, Jean Pierre Lafitte died when an epidemic spread throughout New Orleans, but his son Henry continued in his father's footsteps. Having never married, Henry spent the early years of his life in search of his grandfather's lost treasure. The journey was unsuccessful until one fateful night in December of 1872.

Under a full moon, Henry Lafitte stood on the deck of his sailboat and removed a tattered parchment from his pocket. Tracing his finger along the swampy shoreline of a cove, he designated a small sandy beach for the night's expedition. Grabbing a stubby pencil from behind his ear, he marked the parchment with an X and steered his boat towards the beach.

"This is the spot," he said lightly to himself.

The declaration, however, was not a new thing to the treasure hunter, because his map was riddled with failed expeditions.

Gobs of green moss dripped from the trees, and the night was crisp with a December chill. Through the fog that rested on the water's surface, Henry's sailboat drifted into the sandy beach with a gentle sifting sound. He smiled at the sea of fireflies dancing in the moonlight. Henry Lafitte was filled with the anticipation of discovery.

Walking to the stow box, he grabbed a pickaxe and shovel. Using the tools for balance, he stepped onto the boat's wooden railings and jumped into the shallow waters below. The fog exploded as he plunged towards the sandy shoreline.

Before his feet would find firm ground, however, Henry heard his shovel land with a muffled *THUNK!* beneath the water's surface. Curious, he tilted his head to the side and lifted the shovel into the air before repeating the motion again, and again.

THUNK! THUNK! THUNK!

Henry dropped to his knees. Shooting his hands into the swampy waters around him, he began to search for the source of this mysterious sound. What was it? A rock buried in the sand, or maybe a limb from a fallen tree? Finally, his searching hands gripped onto something. Putting his back into it, Henry pulled with all his might, but his hands slipped and he fell backward into the green water with a splash.

Soaked from head to toe, he quickly rose to his feet and thundered forward. He was embarrassed that he had fallen on his butt, so he grabbed the shovel and hammered away at the mysterious object.

THUNK! THUNK! ... CRACK!

3
SUMMER READING

Despite the chill in the air, sweat oozed from Henry's forehead. He was working hard and his heart raced with the possibilities before him. Drawing his hands from the swampy waters a second time, his eyes discovered what his hands already knew: Henry Lafitte had found his grandfather's lost treasure.

The silver Pieces of Eight weighed heavy in his hands. He could not believe what was happening, and his mind swirled with a flurry of questions. What was so special about tonight? Was it luck? Was it his own fearless determination, like that of his father before him? What made him choose this very spot on this very night? And why had he jumped into the water with the shovel still in his hands? Normally, he would have thrown the tools to the shore before jumping in, but not tonight. What was so different about tonight? Was destiny colliding with reality?

Henry could not answer any of the questions that raced through his mind, because he had dreamed of this moment all of his life. It was finally before him, happening in real time.

Snapping out of his hypnotic experience, he gave in to the excitement rushing through his veins and threw the silver coins high in the air. Gazing upward into the night's sky, he watched the moonlight glisten off the dancing silver that finally plopped into the water around him like heavy raindrops.

Just as the last coin plopped into the water, his ears perked to the distant sound of voices drawing near. Had someone followed him? Would he lose all that he had worked for as fast as he had discovered it? Only time would tell, but Henry Lafitte would not give up without a fight.

∞ ∞ ∞ ∞ ∞ ∞ ∞

I slowly closed the pages of the book. The room was silent. It was so silent I could not even hear the sounds of the other kids shuffling in the beanbags spread across the shag carpet of the library's reading room.

Normally I wouldn't find myself in the library in the middle of summer, reading a textbook, but I liked any story about buried treasure. *Treasure Island* was one of my all-time favorites, but this one was different. This story was about someone who once lived in my hometown, and that was why I was there. Okay, that is not entirely true. The real reason I was sitting in the library on this July 2, right in the middle of my summer vacation, was that I knew Brandy Larson would be there. Brandy was the prettiest girl in school, and even though she barely knew who I was, I liked her.

Every July 2, Ms. Cindi Benson, our town librarian, did a reading of *The Keys of Lafitte,* and Brandy never missed it. Therefore, neither did I. Ms. Benson was cool as librarians go, but sometimes she talked so long without a drink of water that white pockets of spit would form in the corners of her mouth. It was probably a good thing that it was my turn to read from the text. Nobody likes to see gobs of white spit on anyone's mouth, especially a librarian's. My brother told me that my eighth-grade teacher, Mr. Parker, was also a white-pocket-spit talker, but I did not want to think about the coming school year. At that moment, my mind was on buried treasure, and Brandy, of course.

My name is Scott Martin and I'm thirteen years old. I never read unless I had to for school, but this was different. Reading *The Keys of Lafitte* taught me that in the pages of a book you could find adventure. I know it's not the coolest thing to say around other kids, but I did not care. I was now a fan of reading, and that was pretty cool.

The Fourth of July holiday was an exciting event in my hometown. It was exciting not because of the late-night fireworks, and not because of the delicious barbecue, or the homemade vanilla ice cream, either. It was exciting because today was the official start of Pirates Week, which honored our founding father, Jacques Pierre Lafitte, the great-grandson of Jean Lafitte.

Jacques Pierre's life was celebrated because it was rumored that he wanted to continue the legend of his great-grandfather's lost treasure, so he buried all the gold and silver right here in my hometown of Port Townsend, Washington.

According to the story, Henry Lafitte spent most of that fateful night in 1872 unearthing his grandfather's treasure from the dank waters of the swamp. As daylight broke the following morning, he left Barataria Bay, Louisiana, for good. In 1877, at age forty-two, he arrived in the port of Los Angeles, California, where he met Lila Weldon, the woman he would spend the rest of his life with. The two married and settled here in Port Townsend. Thought to become the largest harbor on the west coast, Port Townsend was known as the 'City of Dreams.' Those dreams, however, failed to materialize when the railroad stopped 200 miles short of the city.

In 1900, Henry and Lila gave birth to their only son, Jacques Pierre Lafitte. He was one of our town's founding fathers and whom the book was written about. Named in honor of his great-grandfather, Jacques Pierre grew up uncomfortable with his family legacy. This did not sit well with his father. Henry Lafitte believed that everything in life happened for a reason and that Jacques Pierre should feel honored to bear the Lafitte name. Jacques Pierre, however, was ashamed that his great-grandfather was the ruthless pirate, Jean Lafitte.

During the years following his father's death, Jacques Pierre shied away from public life altogether. Through a team of lawyers, he continued to prosper in the world of business as his father did before him. He built a general store, a movie theater, and even a lumber mill, which became the center of town.

By 1954, a year before his death from lung cancer, Jacques finally made peace with his legacy and began to build the Lafitte Public Library. It was a remarkable construction on the northern end of Town Square, and where I was sitting at the moment.

What made the library so remarkable was the vault located in the basement. Air-conditioned and moisture-controlled, the vault carried first editions of Hemingway, Faulkner and even a first edition of *The Adventures of Tom Sawyer*, signed by Mark Twain himself. The rare book collection was the envy of libraries throughout the state of Washington. My grandfather, Emery, said the Lafitte Public Library put our town on the map, but I still think it was the lost treasure of Jean Lafitte that made my hometown so special.

Inside the rare book vault was yet another vault, which contained four private safe deposit boxes that had belonged to Jacques Pierre Lafitte himself. Rumors traveled fast as people tried to guess the contents of the mysterious boxes, but before anyone could see their contents, he had to find a key by decoding a cipher—which is just a fancy name for a really hard puzzle.

Every year, the estate of Jacques Pierre Lafitte ran a full-page ad in the *Port Townsend Gazette*. The ad detailed the latest clue to the treasure hunt known as the *Keys of Lafitte*. What did the clues look like? Well, to me it was virtually impossible to figure out, because every clue was just another series of seven letters. When added to the clues from previous years, all you had was a long string of mixed-up letters and symbols.

"Does anyone have any questions?" Ms. Benson asked as she placed the textbook back on the shelf. Hands quickly shot up in the reading room as if she was giving away free candy or something.

"Do you think Old Man Sheesley will be the one to find the treasure?" Brandy asked without being called upon.

I even liked the way she talked. Sure, she was beautiful, but hearing her speak was really cool. I often imagined what it would be like if she spoke to me, which, up to now, had not happened. I was not even sure if she knew my name, but that did not matter. To me, she was perfect.

"That's a good question, Brandy," Ms. Benson replied. "Just because Mr. Sheesley found the first two keys, it doesn't mean one of you can't find the third and perhaps the fourth key to the treasure. Anything is possible if you put your mind to it, and I'm sure Town Square is already buzzing with the hope of finding the treasure this weekend."

Brandy was referring to Old Man Sheesley, a local hermit who lived in the Lafitte mansion on the outskirts of town. Ten years ago, in 1962, Old Man Sheesley had solved the first two ciphers of the treasure hunt. Along with the old Lafitte mansion where he lived, which looked a haunted house, Old Man Sheesley was awarded a horse-drawn carriage. Nobody knew the significance of the prizes, but some of the greatest treasure-hunting minds have come to Port Townsend with the hope of making the great discovery, only to come up empty. I could not help but wonder if this would finally be the year that somebody, perhaps one of us sitting right here in this room, would uncover the lost treasure of Jean Lafitte.

As I walked the long marble floor of the library's main hall, I noticed that Brandy was walking in a crowd of other kids behind me. Thinking fast, I stalled at the heavy doors before finally pushing them open for her. When she walked past me, I was certain she had flashed me a fleeting smile. But then, I could not be sure, so I had to find out. Yes, I was about to brave the all-intimidating greeting: *Good morning, Brandy.*

Just as I formed the sentence in my mind, however, somebody grabbed me from behind. It was Tommy Osborne, a bully who had been a thorn in my side for as long as I could remember. He was the most popular kid in school, and perhaps the best baseball pitcher in three counties. This only fueled his ego and made my life more difficult.

"What are you looking at, Dorkster?" he snarled at me.

"Well Tommy, that's what I'm trying to figure out."

"You're real funny, Strikeout King. Didn't you hear the news? Only dorks carry backpacks."

"Wow! Good one!" I shot back with my own dose of sarcasm, which only made Tommy grab my collar and slam me against the massive doors of the library. I could feel the back of my head bounce off the hard wood like a basketball.

"Are you challenging me?" Tommy hissed with venom.

"Mr. Osborne!" Ms. Benson said, arriving behind us in the nick of time. "Don't you have somewhere else to be?"

"Yes, Ma'am," Tommy said, skirting away like a spooked housecat.

Straightening the collar of the ruffled pirate shirt my mom had made, Ms. Benson and I watched Tommy cross over to his gang of thugs near the large fountain in the middle of Town Square.

"You know, Scott," Ms Benson said, turning to me, "sometimes it is better to steer clear of an angry badger, rather than, say, poking him with a stick."

"Yes, Ma'am," I said, agreeing with her. "But not as fun, don't ya think?"

As a smile crept across her aging face, I said my goodbye and exited onto the steps of the grand library, filled with anticipation for the long weekend. The warm morning sun washed over my face. It was a perfect summer day in Port

Townsend, and Ms. Benson was right: Town Square was filled with people dressed in pirate costumes, studying the newspaper ad for the *Keys of Lafitte* treasure hunt. Everyone was dreaming of buried treasure—including me.

As the bell tower at the north end of the library began to chime, I realized this morning's book reading had run longer than I had expected. I was late for meeting my brother at our secret hideout along the banks of the Dungeness River.

Jumping on my bike, I bunny-hopped the curb and rode past the newspaperman selling the morning paper. I snatched a copy from his outstretched hands and flipped him a dime, before he had a chance to yell after me. Tucking the paper into my belt, I pedaled down Water Street, across Sunset Park and through the hole in the fence at the end of Pine Wood Court, which was my secret shortcut to the river. As my feet hammered the pedals of my bike, I had no idea that my life was about to change … forever.

4

THE FORT

I was born ten months after my big brother Gary, and even though most siblings our age did not get along, my brother and I were best friends. Don't get me wrong, we had our disagreements, like the time he told our mom it was my idea to throw bologna on the kitchen ceiling. Hard to believe, but it's true—not about it being my idea, but about bologna sticking to the ceiling.

If you throw a slice of bologna onto the ceiling just right, it will stick like a piece of Velcro because of the suction created by the bologna. Our good friend, John "Zippy" White, holds the record at two minutes and seven seconds of uninterrupted mystery-meat suction. Our family dog, a rambunctious Golden Retriever named Peaches, loves to stand by and wait for the meat to fall from the ceiling. The thing we did not count on, however, were the grease marks left behind by the bologna game. Weeks later, it looked like some suction-cup-footed alien had played a game of hopscotch across the ceiling. This is a bad thing, especially when you have a mom like ours. We spent an entire Saturday afternoon and used a whole bottle of Formula 409 to wash away the rings of grease, but it was worth it. Bologna tossing is the best game ever.

Our dad was a salmon fisherman, and although the *Keys of Lafitte* treasure hunt was a popular event during Pirates Week, our dad said riches only came from an honest day's work. That made sense, but finding buried treasure seemed like a lot more fun than doing chores, if you know what I mean.

During the summer when Dad was away fishing, our friends would come over to help us pull our mom's saltwater taffy. When I was ten years old, my mom got tired of the rising prices of store-bought Halloween candy, so she decided to make her own. Like most everything she did, Mom quickly perfected her efforts, and "Mother's Saltwater Taffy" is now sold to candy shops as far away as New York City. Some thought she was crazy because saltwater taffy was supposed to be a "summer candy," but if you ask any kid in any town, you'll hear that saltwater taffy is good all the time.

Like most kids our age, we spent our summer vacations hanging out at the Boys & Girls Club, playing baseball or dumping quarters into the pinball machine down at Jensen's Ice Cream Parlor on Water Street. We loved to play pinball and eat ice cream, but passed most of our time at our secret fort on the banks of the Dungeness River.

Dug into the riverbank, right next to a fallen tree, our fort was the perfect place to hide from the world. Every kid should have a hiding place like that, especially when he's thirteen years old and trying to make sense of a world that seems to be moving faster and faster with each passing day.

If you did not know where the entrance to our fort was, you could walk right by and not even notice it. That was what made it super cool. It was hidden from the rest of the world, and it was all ours. The roof of the fort was made out of an old car hood covered with dirt and green moss, which seemed to grow everywhere along the Olympic Peninsula. Pieces of driftwood and rounded river rocks were used to build the walls. The plywood floor was covered with a brightly colored rug we'd found in the alley behind the Goodwill Store downtown. We did not know if the rug was being dropped off or had been tossed in a pile to be thrown out, but we strapped it to our bikes and took it anyway. For the most part, we were good kids, but we did fracture an occasional rule here and there.

It was now about 10:30 in the morning, and Gary and I were inside the fort playing a dice game called Dino Board with our friend, Jacqueline Nagle. Jaq, as she liked to be called, lived down the street from our house with her dad. Her mother had died in a car crash when Jaq was in kindergarten, and her dad had never remarried. As a result, it was no surprise that Jaq grew up somewhat of a tomboy. The girl could throw a baseball from center field to second base "on a rope," as we used to call it, which just meant she had a good arm and could throw a line drive to second base without even breaking a sweat. Her talent often placed her on the outside of the popular clique of girls at school. She made it no secret that she'd rather play baseball than with Barbies any day. Jaq was a good friend, perhaps my best friend, and she was the only girl in our club. I only wished the league allowed girls to play baseball, because we could sure use an arm like hers in the outfield.

"Your roll, Jaq," Gary said, looking over the Dino Board. Now this Dino Board was my favorite board game of all. It was a game that taught us how to add up numbers in a variety of ways. A favorite of sailors and fisherman for centuries, the game was really known as Shut the Box, but since this one was hand-crafted by Zippy and his dad, Dino, we called it, the Dino Board.

While I was not a big fan of math, the game was a lot of fun. Built like a wooden treasure box, the Dino Board had nine tiles on the edge, numbered from one to nine. The object of the game was to block out the nine numbered tiles by rolling the dice. See, if you rolled a seven, you could block out the four and three, the five and two, the six and one, or simply turn over the seven tile. Block them all out and you've "Shut the Box." The game ended when you either Shut the Box or could not turn over any more tiles. The lowest total won the game.

Our friend, Jimmy Finn, was sitting in the zebra beanbag behind us. Jimmy was a pudgy, tag-along kid who had a lot to live up to. His big brother, Tracer Finn, was six years older and was the quarterback for the Washington State Cougars. As if that was not enough pressure, Jimmy's father was the sheriff of Port Townsend. Sheriff Dale Finn had also played football when he was young and was the All-American quarterback for Port Townsend High a million years ago. My dad said if it were not for his bad knee, he probably would have been offered a college scholarship and maybe even a chance to play in the NFL.

Dressed in pirate regalia, with an eye patch and a red bandana tied around his scraggly red hair, Jimmy was studying the *Keys of Lafitte* ad in the morning newspaper.

"So, Jimmy … you decode the cipher yet?" Jaq said, turning to face Jimmy as she juggled the dice like a handful of peanuts.

"Who said I was even trying?" Jimmy replied without looking up from his paper. "The new letters make about as much sense as the ones from the last ten years: MO*EHVW. How the heck is anyone supposed to figure out a puzzle with only a bunch of mixed-up letters? I mean, honestly."

"Who knows, maybe Zippy will make an appearance and shed some light on it for us," Jaq said, turning back to me before rolling the dice. "Yes! Double sixes!" she cheered.

"Um, hello? Duh?" Jimmy replied, sticking his nose over the pages of the paper. "It's July second, Jaq. We have a better chance of seeing the Easter Bunny than the likes of Zippy."

"What is with this guy, always with the sarcasm?" Jaq said, smiling at me as she flipped over the five and seven tiles to match her boxcar double sixes.

"Hey, don't blame me that you're such an easy target, Jaq," Jimmy replied.

"Keep talkin', Chunky, and we'll see who's an easy target."

"Woooo, I'm really scared, Jaq," Jimmy said, taunting her as he lifted up his eye patch to shoot her a silly look.

Jaq is not someone you want to mess with. Before Jimmy knew what had happened, Jaq fired one of the dice and nailed him smack-dab in the middle of his forehead. His hand lost its grip on the eye patch, and it snapped shut like a mousetrap.

"Owwwww!" Jimmy screamed.

"Don't blame me that you're such an easy target."

"Quiet," Gary said, lifting his head up from the Dino Board like a gopher coming out of its hole. We craned our necks to listen for an unfamiliar sound, but it was hard to hear anything over the sweet rumbling sound of the river. Our eyes moved around the fort like satellite dishes searching for a signal. Finally, we began to hear something in the distance. It was hard to make out at first, but it got louder and louder with each passing second.

As the sound continued to echo, I began to wonder if Tommy Osborne had followed me from the library. This would be a bad thing, because not only would I receive a fine by the others, but also, our secret hideout would be compromised.

FLIPPITY-FLAPPITY! FLIPPITY-FLAPPITY!

"Jimmy?" Gary turned with eyes of accusation. "Did you break the rules again?

"No way! I stopped. Seriously. I really did," Jimmy replied.

He knew the rules about coming to the secret hideout. Cherry Hill overlooked the river bend where our fort was located. The rule was you had to stop at the top of the hill to make sure nobody was following you. Every fort had rules, and this one was our most important. What good is a secret hideout if outsiders knew about it?

FLIPPITY-FLAPPITY! FLIPPITY-FLAPPITY!

"What the heck is that?" Jimmy asked as the sound grew louder still.

"Whatever it is, it's coming right for us."

FLIPPITY-FLAPPITY!

FLIPPITY-FLAPPITY!

5

FLIPPITY-FLAPPITY

Gary stood at the entrance to the fort like a soldier standing guard outside of a military base. Scanning the area for the mysterious *flippity-flappity* sound was difficult because the hills surrounding the Dungeness River acted like the walls of an echo chamber. It felt like we were being surrounded by this darn *flippity-flappity* sound, which was now attacking us from every angle.

"Over there!" Jaq yelled.

Following her outstretched arm, we watched Zippy race down the Cherry Hill trail. The *flippity-flappity* sound was coming from his bike. *How the heck is that happening?* I wondered. Nobody had a bike that made a sound like that. What was so special about Zippy's bike?

The truth was, Zippy was somewhat of an inventor. He often talked about working with the NASA Space Program one day, and if it were not for his appetite for mischief, the statement would have been somewhat believable. That mischief, I guess, was how he dealt with losing his father in the Vietnam War. His father, Dino White, had been killed when his helicopter was shot down by enemy gunfire. They never recovered his body, and that was hard on Zippy and his mother because all they had to bury was an American flag.

When the news came home that cold morning in January, we began to see less and less of Zippy. He spent most of his after-school time locked away in his dad's workshop, which occupied a small section of their two-car garage. Not only did we see less of him at the fort or down at Jensen's Ice Cream Parlor for pinball, but his all-important batting average on the baseball field was in trouble. This was a bad thing because we were in the middle of the league championship series against our cross-town rivals, the Crab Shack Cardinals. Tommy Osborne was their star pitcher, so you can only imagine how badly I wanted to win.

Zippy wasn't the only one struggling at the plate. My game was in a free-falling slump as well. I was trying to hit a home run—my first home run—which is pretty hard to do, no matter how old you are. Even though I was the shortest, youngest and least experienced player on our team, I was determined to get my home run before the season was over. Tommy had other ideas about giving up a home run to me. It was like he tried extra hard when I stepped into the batter's box.

"Is that sound coming from his bike?" Jaq said, turning to me.

"He's not stopping," Gary said in a revelatory tone of voice.

"That's a fine, you guys. You know it is. Seriously! Fifty cents just like I had to pay last week," Jimmy said, ranting away, which was something he did quite well. Jimmy was happy he would not be the only one to be fined for breaking our most important rule.

"Would you shut up, Jimmy?" Gary snapped, stepping forward. "Something's obviously wrong."

Yes, that's it, I thought. There had to be something wrong, because the whole stopping-on-the-hill-before-you-came-down-to-the-fort thing was Zippy's idea in the first place. It was something he had seen on a television show called *Dragnet.* Whenever an FBI agent wanted to make sure he was not being followed, he would stop, look, and listen to his surroundings. It worked, too, but Zippy was not worried about someone following him today. He was pedaling as fast as he could. Something was indeed wrong.

As he rode closer, another biker emerged out of the trees covering Cherry Hill. It was Harrison Tweed, the newest member of our club and somewhat of an odd duck, if you asked me. Harrison had these buck teeth that were so bucked, the kid could eat a watermelon through a chain link fence.

Harrison's family had moved to town a few months ago, and the guy desperately tried to fit in, but with a name like Harrison and those darned bucked teeth, he was certain to be on the outside of any "in crowd." His father, a big-shot lawyer of some kind, recognized his son's social dysfunction and made sure he was included in the Jefferson County Little League. Because they lived on the other side of town, Harrison was placed on the Crab Shack Cardinals team by the league.

Tommy's father, Coach Mike Osborne, refused to add Harrison to his team, but when Frank Marquette, a bench-warming second baseman for the Cardinals, moved to Santa Monica, California, Coach Osborne had to agree. League rules stated each team needed at least twelve players. I'm surprised Harrison did not have splinters in his butt, because he rode that bench more than a jockey rides a racehorse. The truth was, Harrison did not fit in with the other guys on his team, which is probably why he fit in so well with us.

We liked to think our little club was cool, but we were far from it. Well, maybe Gary was cool a little bit, but we all knew we were different. We just were not like other kids; but in hindsight, I think that was what made us cool. We were different and did not care about fitting in. Dad said that one of the biggest secrets of life was loving yourself in your own "different-ness." Yeah, sure, it takes guts, but who wants to be like someone else? I liked who I was, and I loved being different.

Arriving in a rush, Zippy power-slid off his bike in one motion. His sneakers dug into the moist ground like a farmer's heavy plow. Harrison was right behind him, and both of them were dressed like pirates. Harrison was wearing one of those store-bought pirate costumes you could get during Halloween. Ours were handmade by Mom, which made them cool in my opinion. Yeah, they were super cool, actually.

"You guys aren't going to believe this!" Zippy said, out of breath as he walked over to the edge of the river. Pulling on a rope tied to a large metal stake that we had hammered into the ground, he retrieved our club's secret cold soda stash. Here's the thing about the Dungeness River: no matter what time of year it was, the water coming from the Olympic Mountains was so cold it could turn you blue in a matter of seconds.

Popping off the top of a Dr. Pepper bottle, Zippy chugged down the sweet, sugary soda in a single gulp. Wiping his lips with the puffy sleeve of his pirate shirt, he let out one of his famous soda burps before looking over at Jimmy.

"What the heck happened to you?" said Zippy.

"What do you mean?" Jimmy asked.

"Your forehead. Did you sleep on a dice or something? You got a number three right there!" Zippy pressed his index finger on Jimmy's dented forehead.

"What?" Jimmy asked, feeling the lump on his forehead that had grown when Jaq had hit him with the dice. When Harrison started to laugh, Jimmy quickly turned on him. "What are *you* laughing at, Cardinal scum?" he barked with anger in his eyes. "You're lucky to even be here. Come to think of it, why *is* he here?"

"Because I stopped to get him, Jimmy," Zippy replied, defending Harrison. "You got a problem with that?"

"Yeah, Chubby, who died and made you boss?" Harrison said, stepping from his bike, challenging Jimmy. Even though Harrison was an outcast on his own baseball team, hanging out with us gave him a small shred of confidence. The fact that Zippy liked Harrison more than he liked Jimmy did not help Jimmy's cause, either.

"Um, hello? Is it my imagination or doesn't this guy play for the enemy?"

"We've been over this, Jimmy," Gary added quickly. "He's one of us."

"Why am I the only one who thinks this is wrong? He plays for the enemy! He could be a spy, stealing our base running signs!"

Jimmy worried about everything. If a mosquito landed on his arm, he was certain malaria or yellow fever would soon follow. It was quite funny, actually.

"Quit being so paranoid, Jimmy, or you're gonna get that tumor you keep talking about," Zippy said, continuing to rib him with a laugh.

"Paranoia doesn't give you tumors," Jimmy said, trying to convince himself of the statement before looking to Gary for answers. "Right, Gary?"

"No, but being a jerk does."

"Oh, so now it's my fault?"

Deflecting the argument, I turned my attention to Zippy's bike. "Man! How'd you make your bike have that sound, Zip? That's bosso-keeno."

"Pretty cool, huh?" Zippy said, showing off the clothes-pinned playing cards in the spokes of his back wheel. "Kinda sounds like a motor, doesn't it? My uncle Alan showed it to me last night. I guess he and my dad used to do it when they were kids. What do you think?"

"I think I need to get some clothespins and *get my motor runnin'*," I said, beginning to sing the Steppenwolf hit song, "Born to Be Wild." Jaq quickly joined in the singing and played a bit of air guitar for added flair.

> *"Head out on the highway,*
> *Lookin' for adventure ..."*

"All right, knock it off," Gary said, trying to stay focused.

But Jaq and I would not be denied the amazing chorus on the hit song, which had become popular well before our time.

> *"For whatever comes our way.*
> *BORN TO BE WILLLLLD!"*

"I said, knock it off!" Gary turned to us with a scowl.

"Come on, G. Don't be such a dud. I love that song," I cut in, continuing the chorus as if I were auditioning for the school's talent show.

"BORN TO BE ... WILLLLLD!"

I slowly stopped singing because everyone was looking at me like I was a complete goober. At that moment, I kind of felt like one, so I nudged Jaq as if to say, 'You left me hangin' there.' My awkward spotlight finally ended as Gary looked at Zippy with concern.

"What's going on?"

"Yeah, Zip?" Jaq added. "What aren't we going to believe?"

"I solved it, man!" Zippy said, finishing off his Dr. Pepper with a final, juicy-sounding burp.

"Solved what?"

"The third cipher. I think I found the location of the lost treasure," Zippy replied, as he pulled out the morning's full-page *Keys of Lafitte* newspaper ad from his backpack.

We all carried backpacks because we never knew what the day's adventure might bring or what supplies we might need. In my backpack were a few important things, like a good flashlight, a pocketknife, a bag of trail mix, which our dad liked to call "gorp" for whatever reason, a few firecrackers and a stash of my mom's saltwater taffy. Here's the thing about carrying a backpack. It opened us up for all sorts of ridicule from the older kids. We were called everything from "bookworms" to Tommy's favorite cut-down of all, "dorks." I think Zippy rationalized it best when he talked about carrying around a backpack: "I'd rather have it and not need it, than need it and not have it."

Until I heard a better reason not to carry a backpack, I took Zippy's advice and carried one.

Gary was all business. He turned to Zippy and asked him what he was talking about.

"I think I know where the lost treasure of Jean Lafitte is buried."

Those astonishing words, said by Zippy, were hard to believe. The idea that we, a bunch of misfits, would ever find the lost treasure of Jean Lafitte was unthinkable, but our eyes widened nonetheless. The excitement shooting through my veins was like the energy of a cannonball fired from a pirate ship.

TREASURE TIP

Never wish you were someone else.
If you were another person, who would be you?

6

A CLOSER LOOK

"**I** don't see why we can't just skip the whole *Keys of Lafitte* thing this year," Jimmy said, grumbling more than talking, which was normal for the complainer. "It's just a bunch of mixed-up letters and a waste of time."

"Look who woke up with poopie diapers this morning," Jaq said, ribbing Jimmy.

"Honestly. Even my dad said the treasure was a big fat dead end."

"Yeah, then your dad is a big fat dud, because with the addition of this morning's letter combination, I think

I solved the third cipher," Zippy insisted with his nose buried in the newspaper ad.

"Oh yeah? Well, at least I have a dad."

I don't think Jimmy really understood what he was saying when he said it, but Gary made sure he did in a flash as he put Jimmy into a special headlock he had learned from his martial arts class down at the YMCA. I felt bad for Jimmy because I could see Gary was really cranking down hard with the headlock.

"Eeeeowwww!"

"Say you're sorry."

"Eeeeowwww!" Jimmy squealed. "You're pinching my neck. Okay. Okay. I'm sorry. Jeez!" Jimmy said, rubbing his neck as Gary released his vice grip-like hold.

Our eyes quickly shot over to Zippy, wondering how he would react to Jimmy's bone-headed comment, but there was nothing. Not even the slightest bit of sarcasm, which was odd for Zippy who had a forked tongue for cut-downs, especially when Jimmy was involved. Those two were like oil and water sometimes, always quick with comebacks and cut-downs. Zippy, however, at this moment, remained silent.

When anyone brought up the subject of family, Zippy would go quiet, which is understandable. Maybe he thought if he did not talk about his dad dying, it did not happen. I don't think any of us is very good at talking about our feelings, but my mom always said, "When you keep something that hurts welled up inside, it just makes it hurt longer."

It was hard to worry about Zippy, because my mind was racing with possibilities. The thought of us possibly uncovering the lost treasure of Jean Lafitte was so awesome I could not contain myself. I was certain we would get our pictures in the paper and be rich beyond our wildest dreams. We could buy new bikes and maybe even buy the river where our fort was located. That would be cool.

Putting the awkward moment behind us, we gathered around as Zippy spread the newspaper over the large river rock we would sunbathe on when the weather was warm. The full-page ad was the same ad we had seen for most of our lives, or as far back as we could remember. This was the headline:

THE KEYS OF LAFITTE
Solve the Cipher! Find Lafitte's Lost Treasure!
*MO*EHVW*

There was a small paragraph under the drawing of a giant alder tree. It told the history of Jacques Pierre Lafitte and the treasure hunt, but it also had a short, detailed section about Old Man Sheesley and his discovery of the first two keys.

The third cipher was a string of seventy-seven mixed-up letters laid out across the root system of the penciled drawing of the giant tree. For years, people thought this meant the treasure was somehow buried under a tree, but until the cipher was solved, nobody could be sure. With the addition of the seven new letters from this morning's newspaper, the third cipher looked like this:

*Oppcogwdavpyvvrqesielcmrtael*amyne*kjzm,*
*wtfkzzzfaffjoppervsnccp*rragmo*ehvw*

"All right, tell me what you see," Zippy said, sounding like a piano teacher asking a group of first-year students to play Beethoven or something.

"Um, I see a bunch of mixed-up letters," Jaq said.

"Yeah, Zip. It might as well be written in Latin," I said, agreeing with Jaq, which I often did. Maybe it was because she was the only girl and I was the youngest, but Jaq and I were best friends.

"This is lame. I'm goin' to see Fatman for some ice cream," Jimmy said, pulling the eye patch from his face. "Fatman" was Harley Jensen, owner of Jensen's Ice Cream Parlor on Water Street and the sponsor of our baseball team. Harley was enormous. In his late thirties, Fatman was about two Ding Dongs shy of 300 pounds. He was one of the coolest adults in town, and we shared a common enemy: the Osborne family. According to Fatman, Tommy's father, Mike Osborne, had picked on him when he was our age. Seems like bullies raise bullies and cool parents raise cool kids. I was glad I was in the latter group.

"Suit yourself," Zippy replied, "but if you leave now, don't expect us to share any of the buried treasure with you."

Jimmy froze. He had not thought of that possibility, but after a beat of consideration, he swung his leg over the Mongoose bike his parents had bought him for his thirteenth birthday. Chrome plated with moon-taped lettering, the bike still had that new bike shine. Jimmy was not the most active kid in town. His bulging belly attested to that.

"Look man," he said, turning to Zippy, "I think it's great you puttin' your time into something and all, and I'm sorry about what I said about your dad and stuff. But Zippy ... people have been lookin' at that stupid puzzle for over ten years. People older *and* a heck of a lot smarter than all of us combined. Some people spend all year tryin' to figure it out. But what? You eat two bowls of Wheaties this morning and suddenly you think you're this super-smart dude who's gonna solve the cipher? Honestly."

"Wow! Get a listen to *big brain* Jimmy," Jaq said. "Big boy is using words way out of his league."

"Whatever, Jaq," Jimmy said, keeping an eye out for any flying dice she might retaliate with.

"No big whoop," Zippy replied with a smile as he ran his hand over the newspaper ad to flatten the crumpled edges. "If Jimmy here wants to miss out having his picture in the paper, that's up to him."

Zippy turned away from Jimmy and focused on the newspaper before him. "All right, let's get to work. The first key reward was a useless New Orleans horse-drawn carriage, and the second key reward was the old Lafitte mansion. We know that Jacques Pierre was the great-grandson of Jean Lafitte."

"So?" someone asked.

"So, all this got me thinking. New Orleans? France?"

"Hold on! Wait a minute. Are you tellin' me the cipher suggests we head to France?" Gary asked.

"I didn't say that."

"Then what are you saying?"

"If you allow me to continue …"

"Well, you're not making any sense."

"It's a recap."

"No, it's confusing. When you talk all weird and stuff, it's hard to follow. Just say what you're going to say, and let's get on with it, Zip," Gary ordered him.

"My father always said the best way to get where you're going is to know where it was you came from. I'm just stating what we already know."

"Then tell us what we *need* to know."

"I'm trying. Look, I'm just saying all that stuff, the first and second cipher—who was involved—it all got me thinking about the third cipher. And since they always

print the results of the last cipher in an ad for the next
cipher, I'm drawing a conclusion that the ciphers are
related, which is probably why Old Man Sheesley found
the first two. Find one, you have a better chance at finding
the next one."

Gary rolled his eyes because Zippy was at it again. He
often talked high falutin', you know, over your head to
show how smart he was. It was not like he was trying
to make us feel dumb or anything—he just had a social
handicap of making sense in his mind. But somewhere
between his mind and his mouth, the message became so
jumbled that nobody could understand it. That was Zippy.

"Okay, look. When I saw this year's clue of MO*EHVW,
I went back to the beginning and did some research on
ciphers in the *World Book Encyclopedia* before breakfast—"

"—you were reading the *World Book Encyclopedia* before
breakfast? Are you crazy?" Jaq said, cutting him off with a
dose of sarcasm.

"What's wrong with that?" Zippy asked.

"Zip, let's go. Wrap it up," Gary urged.

"I don't think I'm the first to research ciphers where
the *Keys of Lafitte* is concerned, but I found out there was
only one cipher ever invented by the French. It's called the
Vigenère cipher. This Blaise de Vigenère guy, whatever
his name is, was some sixteenth century diplomat, and the
cipher he invented is just like the cipher Old Man Sheesley
solved."

"Zip!" Gary said, growing more impatient.

"How's it work?" I asked, reaching out to Gary to ease
up on Zippy.

"I'm glad you asked."

"Why?"

"What?"

"Why are you glad I asked?" I said with a straight face.

Zippy stalled for a second then started to explain what he meant before we all broke out laughing. This was our way of messin' with Zippy and the way he talked.

"Ah, funny. Real funny," he said, taking offense. "You're gonna be laughin' hard when I take the map home and find this puppy without you."

"A puppy? Did anyone say puppy?" Jaq joked with him, which got us all laughing, so I turned to Jaq.

"Why yes, Jaq. I'm glad you asked."

Gary finally reeled us in and asked Zippy to continue.

"The Vigenère cipher changes the value of N."

"Yeah, and people tried that already," Harrison said, leaning in. "You encode your message with a pass-phrase, and the letters of your pass-phrase determine how each letter in the message is encrypted based on the letter N, right?"

"Right, the pass-phrase determines the value of N," Zippy said, looking up at Harrison. "I didn't know you were into this stuff."

"What else is there to do in this town?" Harrison said, laughing slightly.

"Other than baseball?" I said, defending my favorite pastime.

"So what did you find out?"

"My father always said when you're creating something and you get lost, all you have to do is go back to the beginning and start over."

"Yeah, Zip. You already said that."

"Well, I started looking into the life of Jean Lafitte. I read about his wife and anything to do with his son, Jean Pierre Lafitte."

"Jean Lafitte wasn't married," I stated, happy that I had something to contribute other than sarcasm.

"You're right, he wasn't," Zippy said. "Jean Pierre Lafitte was an illegitimate child. But then it occurred to me—Jean Pierre's mother had the last name of Villars. I concluded that it had to be the pass-phrase."

"You lost me, Zip," Jaq said, looking up from the newspaper ad.

"Me, too," Gary added.

"Look, with Villars as the pass-phrase, the Vigenère cipher decodes this gobbledygook of letters into this!" Zippy pulled out a piece of notebook paper from his backpack.

Theropeiskeyedwithinthegiantfencetree,
liftherupforthetreasurerailedthee.

"Looks like more gobbledygook letters," I said.

"Yeah? Well, watch this." Zippy pulled out a pen from his pocket. Hunkering over the notebook paper, he began to draw slashes between the letters until we finally saw this:

The/rope/is/keyed/within/the/giant/*fence*/tree/
lift/her/up/for/the/treasure/*railed*/thee

I could not believe it. At thirteen years old, Zippy had made sense out of something that had stumped people of all ages for over ten years. The accomplishment was indeed a victory for every kid in town, but as the celebration of the moment was crossing my mind, I could not help but wonder what the decoded cipher meant. All we really had were the two short sentences that felt more like an incomplete poem than a clue to the lost treasure of Jean Lafitte.

With my mind focused on questions like this, and others like it, I was unable to comprehend what happened next. Never in a million years would I have seen it coming, but it did. And it caught us all by surprise.

7

THE MEANING

"The rope is keyed within the giant fence tree—lift her up for the treasure railed thee," Zippy read aloud.

"That doesn't even make sense," Jimmy said from the seat of his bike.

"Yeah, and I thought you went to get ice cream."

Gary did not want Jimmy and Zippy to start another one of their back and forth debates, so he turned the piece of notepaper around, attempting to make sense of the code. "A giant fence tree? What the heck is that, Zip?"

"Yeah, Zip," Jaq added. "I'm more confused now than when the letters were all jumbled up.

"That's okay. Just look at how the words 'fence' and 'railed'—"

"—have stars next to 'em?" Jimmy said, finishing Zippy's sentence.

"They're called asterisks, Dill Weed," Harrison chimed in with his own two cents.

"So what's it mean?"

"At first I thought they were clues. You know, like the treasure was buried inside a fence near the train tracks or something."

"Train tracks?"

"Then I discovered this," Zippy said, pulling out the *World Book Encyclopedia* from his backpack. Flipping through the pages, he quickly found what he was looking for. A smile crept across his face as if he was looking at a picture of an old friend. Turning the book around, he cradled it in his arms. His finger slapped down on the thin pages of the encyclopedia to show us the bold heading at the top of the page: *Railfence Cipher.*

"No way!" we all gasped collectively.

"Jimmy, get me the map of the Dungeness River. It's on the rock shelf behind the beanbag in the fort," Zippy ordered.

"Why do I have to get it?" he squealed.

"Would you just go and stop complaining?" Gary said, giving him a shove.

"What are you picking on me for?" he squealed again. "What did I do?"

"Go!" we all shouted in unison.

As Jimmy kicked a rock and shuffled to the fort, Zippy grabbed his notepad, and we all peered in for a closer look at the cipher.

T o s e t t i * c r l h p t r u r e h
h r p i k y d i h n h g a t f n e t e, i t e u f r h t e s r * a l d t e.
e e e w i e n e * e f r o e a e i * e

I still did not understand what he was doing until Jimmy returned with the map and Zippy spread it open on the large rock. We all huddled around like a football team listening to their quarterback call out the next play.

"What exactly are we looking for?" Jaq asked Zippy, but he did not answer. He was quietly talking to himself as he worked things out, something he often did. We looked at each other with blank stares, trying to act like we knew what was going on, but we did not. In fact, we had no clue of what was going on, so we just watched Zippy place the decoded Railfence Cipher over the map like a sheet of tracing paper.

"If my calculations are correct, the asterisks should line up to the ..." Zippy's voice began to trail off. He spun the map in a few directions, matching different landmarks with the asterisks of the decoded cipher. Finally, he leaned back in defeat.

"What's wrong?" Gary looked at him.

"It doesn't work."

"What do you mean it doesn't work?" Jaq said, perking up.

"I mean it doesn't work," he said, grabbing the map. "The cipher mentions a giant tree. Biggest tree I know of is the Sullivan Tree." Zippy pointed to a giant tree just up the river from where we were. It was known as the Sullivan Tree because Billy Sullivan, a kid five years older than we were once took a dare from his friends and went down the Dungeness River in the inner tube of a semi-truck tire. It was a dare because not only was the water freezing, but you'd also have to be an idiot to attempt the stunt with all the twists and turns of the river. Sullivan made it through the upper Dungeness just fine, but he slammed into the biggest tree on the entire river. Since then, he's moved away to college, but everyone knew about the Sullivan Tree, and if you looked close enough, you could see the indentation of Billy Sullivan's face right there in the bark. He was one ugly kid.

Zippy continued, indicating spots on the map. "I thought if we lined up the first asterisks to the old Sullivan tree at the river bend here ..." He pointed at a spot on the map. "... and lined up the second asterisks to the left field fence of Sunset Park, here ..." He pointed again. "... it might—"

"It might what?" I asked quickly.

"It might show the location of the third key, but it doesn't. I was wrong." Zippy turned to Jimmy. "So go ahead and say it."

"Say what?" Jimmy replied, meekly.

"I know you're just dying to rub it in my face, so go ahead and say it. Say that this whole stupid thing was a hoax!" Zippy began to fume with frustration. "I wish I never would've wasted all that time with my dad on this stupid thing. I wish I'd never heard about Jean Lafitte and his stupid lost treasure! Ever!"

Zippy climbed to his feet and fired a rock against the Sullivan Tree. Another, then another, until he finally fell to his knees, surrendering to the tears that had been brewing ever since his dad had died.

At that moment we all knew this was not about finding the third key to the treasure. This was about a family tradition he had had with his father as far back as we could remember. Every Pirates Week, when the new clue appeared in the newspaper, Zippy and his dad would spend days in their garage, devouring clues and trying new ideas to discover the location of the lost treasure of Jean Lafitte.

Suddenly, we were enveloped in a blanket of awkward silence. Nobody knew what to do, or what to say, for that matter. We wanted to make the hurt go away, but nobody could do that. Zippy's dad was gone, and he was never coming back.

This got me to thinking about Gary and me. Grandpa Emery always told us that what happens in your childhood shapes your tomorrow. As I watched Zippy cry on the bank of the Dungeness River, I had something of a revelation about my own life. Although our dad spent big chunks of time away catching king salmon, Gary and I always knew he was coming home. Zippy's dad was never coming home. There would be no more baseball games, fishing trips or Christmas mornings together. No more games of catch in the front yard and no more barbecues on Saturday afternoons—only memories of days gone by. This made me sad for Zippy. It made me sad for anyone who had ever lost anyone.

"What happens if you take out those two words?" Harrison said, hunched over the decoded cipher text.

"What two words?" Gary asked, joining him.

"These two words here. The ones with the asterisks."

"Would you just forget it? Okay? Just forget it!" Zippy was now annoyed.

"Come on, Zip. Take a look," Jaq suggested, joining us.

"Seriously," Gary continued, "the two words that led you to the Railfence Cipher—Harrison's right, they don't fit."

"Yeah, Zip. What do you think about decoding the cipher without the two words?" I added.

It was obvious we were trying to get his mind off of his father, but Harrison was really onto something. After a quick beat of consideration, Zippy crossed back over to us and got to work. Striking out the two words, he laid the new decoded cipher text over the map and lined it up to the Sullivan Tree. It worked! The new decoded cipher text produced an "X" between the Sullivan Tree and another large tree along the river. Our mouths collectively dropped open for a long beat.

"X marks the spot," I whispered. We had found it.

TREASURE TIP

Every day is a gift.
That's why it's called the present.

8

X MARKS THE SPOT

Between the Sullivan Tree and the next tree, a third and much larger tree had fallen into a deep section of the Dungeness River. The X was directly over the exposed root system of the fallen tree, just as the ad displayed in the newspaper.

Was the third key buried somewhere in the exposed root system? If it was, how long had the tree been upended? Could the third key be underwater on the riverbed? Before I had a chance to think about the answers to the questions that raced through my mind, a piercing whistle shattered our moment of discovery.

My gaze turned upward to Harrison in slow motion. His two index fingers were lodged in his mouth and his cheeks were puffed out so far that he looked like the famous trumpet player, Louis Armstrong, playing his trumpet on a New Orleans street corner. I blinked slowly as the piercing whistle continued to attack my ears. Then I saw them coming out of the trees like a battalion of soldiers executing an ambush. It was Tommy Osborne and three of his thug Cardinal teammates.

Jimmy was right. Harrison had doubled-crossed us. When our attention turned to the approaching enemy, Harrison grabbed the map from Zippy's hands and scrambled up the embankment to join Tommy. The way he handed the map to Tommy suddenly made me feel sorry for Harrison. I knew Tommy had manipulated Harrison's weak personality. Harrison was so desperate to be accepted by the "cool kids," he had sold out the friends he had.

"That doesn't belong to you, Osborne!" Zippy shouted.

"Too bad, so sad—Dork! Possession's nine-tenths of the law." Tommy laughed like the ruthless villain he was.

"Yeah, dork," Harrison said, nudging Tommy as he used the same knock against Zippy. "If it wasn't for me, you'd still be on the rocks crying your eyes out like a little baby."

Zippy's blood was about to boil over. I could see it. While he was not the thug type, I was confident he could have taken Harrison in a fight, but for what? A bruised ego? For a treasure map, which at this point was still unproven? Fights were never worth it. I'd rather mop the baseball field with 'em than risk getting into a fight.

"Easy, Zip, he's not worth it," I said, trying to calm him.

"I'm gonna kill him," Zippy grumbled.

"Remember guys, the best revenge is living well," Jimmy offered. We all turned around to look at him as if to say, "*What* are you talking about?"

"What are you looking at? That's what I've always heard," he said, shrugging one of his shoulders into the air.

As Tommy and his crew quickly studied the map, Jaq turned to the rest of us. "What are we going to do now? They have the map!"

"I got a plan." Zippy said, almost to himself.

"Well, this plan of yours had better include the powers of a fortune teller, Zip, 'cause they got the map," Gary said, frustrated.

"In my backpack there's a bag of M-80s I made last week for the Fourth of July picnic. It should be right next to my slingshot," Zippy said slowly over his shoulder to Gary.

"Mortar fire," Gary said, smiling. "I like it."

"Scooter? Jaq? I'm gonna need your arms."

"For what?"

"When I make a dash for the fallen tree, I need you guys to cover me."

"With what?" I asked incredulously.

"What do you think you're standing on, a bed of marshmallows?" Zippy replied, indicating the rocks under our feet. The rocks of the Dungeness River had a common characteristic—they were round and smooth from the years of river flow, which made them perfect for throwing.

Zippy continued. "I don't know what I'm lookin' for, so I need you and Jaq to buy me some time. Gary? Make sure you keep 'em away from that fallen tree no matter what, all right?"

"Bombs away."

"What about me?" Jimmy said, sounding left out.

"You're with me. If anyone's following me, you need to take 'em out."

"What do you mean 'take 'em out'? Take 'em out how? I've never taken anyone out," Jimmy said, knowing he was anything but the enforcer type.

"You might as well go home, losers. We got the map," Tommy announced.

Watching each of us slowly prepare for the execution of Zippy's plan, Tommy began to sense something was up. When Zippy suddenly took off running, Tommy reacted.

"The fallen tree!" Tommy yelled to his thugs. "The key's buried at the base of the fallen tree! Go! Go! Go!"

Everyone sprang into action, but Zippy had a fifty-yard head start on two thick-necked bullies named Joe and Chris Amato. Though they had badger-like necks, the Amato twins were the fastest baseball players around. The only chance you had for a base hit against these guys was a line drive into the gap, but even then they could chase it down and hold your line drive to a single.

Jimmy was lagging behind, but offered a diversion when the shortest kid in Tommy's crew, Danny "The Vacuum" Simon, dumped his bike in the bushes and tried to cut off Zippy. Danny was called "The Vacuum" because at shortstop his tiny legs and catlike reflexes enabled him to suck up any base hit between second and third base. He was a great player. Unfortunately for us, he was on the other team.

Although the Crab Shack Cardinals were the defending league champions, we had miraculously taken game one of the championship series. All we had to do was win tonight's game and we'd be crowned Jefferson County League Champions. If we lost, there would be a third and final game before the Fourth of July picnic. But we could not think about any of that right now. We were fighting for what was rightfully ours. We were fighting for buried treasure, and this was war.

Danny whizzed past Jimmy and made a beeline towards Zippy and the fallen tree. Kneeling down, I grabbed the first rock my fingers touched and fired it side-armed at

Danny Simon's feet. It was a perfect throw, and it stopped him dead in his tracks. He thought about picking up a rock and returning fire, but he continued to run after Zippy.

The Amato twins were dancing across the rocky shore like a couple of antelope on the open range in Montana, gaining on Zippy with every stride. Jimmy, on the other hand, was already out of breath and slowed to a jog.

Gary placed a homemade M-80 into the leather catch of the slingshot and lit the fuse. Pulling back, he took aim at Tommy and Harrison as they made their way down the embankment.

The lit M-80 sailed into the air and landed five feet in front of them. Their eyes widened and before they could react.

KABOOM!

It was like watching a war movie on television, the way the M-80 tore into the earth like mortar fire. The blast was louder than a normal M-80. It was so loud that everyone turned to look—everyone but Zippy, who had finally arrived at the fallen tree.

"What did you put in these things?" Gary yelled over to Zippy.

"Keep firing!" Zippy shouted as he began to move rocks away from the base of the tree, digging into the sandy shoreline for the treasure.

I never would have thought of hitting anyone with the tangerine-sized river rocks beneath my feet, but I could not say the same for Jaq. She was firing rocks with bad intentions.

WHACK!

To nobody's surprise, Jaq nailed Joe Amato right above the kneecap as he raced after Zippy. I winced when I saw the rock slam into his leg, because Jaq threw nothing but fastballs.

Going down hard, Joe grabbed his leg and rolled back and forth, screaming in pain. His brother, Chris, immediately stopped to help. If I had not known any better, I would have said Jaq's throw made Joe start to cry.

Danny Simon and Tommy, followed closely by Harrison, arrived at the toppled tree just behind Zippy.

"Spread out and start digging!" Tommy ordered.

"You got no right to be here, Osborne," Zippy said, burrowing into the ground like a dog after a gopher. "I'm the one who solved the cipher."

"That's a lie," Harrison snapped back at Zippy. "I was the one who solved the cipher, and you know it."

As they began to debate back and forth while digging into the dark sand of the riverbank, Gary lit another M-80 bomb.

Pulling back the slingshot, he aimed for Harrison who was off to the side.

"What are you doing? Zippy's down there!" I said.

"Relax, I'm just gonna give 'em something to think about."

The lit M-80 whizzed past our ears as it took flight, tumbling end over end. From the looks of the trajectory, it looked like a pretty good shot, but suddenly a gust of wind blew through the canyon and changed the M-80's flight path. It hit Tommy on top of the head and bounced inside of the hallowed-out section of the tree next to them.

"Uh oh," Gary said.

"Uh oh? What do you mean, uh oh?" I asked.

"Look out!" Gary yelled out after his misfire. Zippy stood up with dirt on his hands, not sure what was happening.

Tommy, Harrison and Danny Simon looked around and followed the sizzling sound of the burning fuse, which hissed like an angry snake inside of the partially hollowed-out tree.

KAAAAA–BOOOOOOM!

The compression of the small space inside the trunk of the tree increased the power of the already powerful M-80. It was an impressive sight as the tree split in half. The sound was deafening. It was the same sound I had heard when loggers cut down the giant trees behind our house—cracking and splintering. The tree tore apart like a piece of hardened beef jerky.

Looking up, Zippy saw the larger portion of the tree beginning to fall right above him. Thinking fast, he dove for cover, but was suddenly upended when something rose from the ground under his feet.

Lifting large rocks into the air like tiny marbles, a cable, fastened to the inside of the giant blown-apart tree, raced past Tommy, flew past Harrison, tripped Danny Simon as he tried to dodge it and, finally, slipped into the water, which shot up into the air like the fountain in Town Square.

As the mysterious cable sped into the river, a second cable began to rip through the years of overgrown bark of the Sullivan Tree, racing to a limb high above. The giant limb fell onto the bank, and the cables suddenly drew taught, causing a catapult effect, which lifted a small wooden box—a treasure chest about the size of a fishing tackle box—from the bottom of the river.

The treasure chest swung high in the air and finally came to rest, suspended by the cables, some twenty feet over our heads. Water dripped down from inside the ancient chest. Everyone stood in amazement, not quite sure of what had happened during the last fifteen seconds of our lives. Whatever it was, it was fascinating. It was every kid's dream to find buried treasure, and we had definitely found something.

Questions began to fly through my head as fast as the flapping wings of a hummingbird. Was the cable buried under the riverbed a booby trap to keep treasure hunters away? Was the contraption built for situations like this, in which two treasure-hunting parties arrived at the discovery simultaneously? And what was inside the chest dangling high above our heads?

Of course, it had to be the third key to Jean Lafitte's treasure, but would there be anything else along with it? Maybe it was a chest of gold or maybe a cache of silver Pieces of Eight? How would we get the chest down before Tommy and his thugs got to it? Time would only tell.

TREASURE TIP

*Real friends like you for who you are,
not what you can do for them.*

9

THE MYSTERY BOX

I already knew Tommy was a great athlete, but watching him race up the Sullivan Tree towards the mysterious treasure chest made me wonder—not about how good he was at sports and all things athletic, but about my own abilities and my place in the world.

I was not popular by any stretch of the imagination. I was, at best, an ordinary kid trying to fit in. This kind of thinking was nothing new for me. I had been playing this mental ping-pong game most of my life. Questions like, "Why did it have to be like this?" were normal for me. It was not just one question, either. My mind would become polluted with so much self-doubt that it was hard to think clearly." Why was I born so short?" "Why didn't I have the natural talent to be great at sports?" It was nonstop, but I was certain that if I could be better at sports like Tommy, I could get the attention of Brandy Larson.

The Amato twins stood guard at the base of the Sullivan Tree, practically daring any of us to climb it. It did not matter that we outnumbered them, either. Nobody in their right mind wanted any part of the Amato twins and their badger-like necks. Except for Zippy. He darted past Danny Simon, ducked under Harrison's outstretched hands and arrived at the giant limb lying on the riverbank. Yes! It was the next logical choice, because the other end of the steel cable holding the treasure chest was fastened to that limb. Maybe if we could shake the cable, the chest would fall before Tommy was able to get to it.

Looking up, I knew we had to hurry because Tommy was leaning onto the cable for the treasure chest. Luckily, it was just out of his reach. In order to grab the chest, Tommy would have to shimmy his way onto the cable, and from my vantage point, that was not going to be an easy task.

"Careful, Tommy," Danny said, craning his neck upward.

Tommy worked his hands like an inchworm on the cable. "I'm not sure going to the emergency room today is such a good idea!" one of the Amato Twins shouted, but Tommy was not listening. He was focused on the treasure chest before him.

Jaq, Jimmy, Gary and I ran to help Zippy with the fallen limb, but it was too heavy to budge. When Jaq saw that Tommy was getting closer to the treasure chest, she grabbed the cable and shook it back and forth. One of

Tommy's hands slipped and the cable slapped across his chest, stopping his fall. He quickly reached back for the safety of the tree and shouted down at Jaq.

"Hey man, what are you trying to do, kill me?"

"That's the idea!" Jaq shouted back to him.

"Too bad, so sad—Osborne!" Zippy screamed. Like anyone, Zippy hated to lose, especially to these guys. So there we were, at an impasse. We were not about to let Tommy get onto the cable, and they were not about to let us climb up the Sullivan Tree.

Feeling helpless, Gary picked up a rock and threw it at the chest, but it sailed past without hitting anything. "Don't just stand there," he said, "Grab a rock and let's bust it open."

"We don't know what that box is made of," Jimmy replied.

"Well, I'm not going to sit here and watch that guy get *our* treasure."

With Tommy inching himself onto the cable again, the treasure chest became a moving target, which made the throw even more difficult. Looking back, I saw Jaq grab the slingshot from Gary's back pocket. Kneeling down, she found a small river rock and loaded it into the slingshot's catch. Pulling back, she took aim and fired.

SMACK!

The rock hit the treasure chest dead on and we heard the small wooden treasure chest crack. Although it had been her idea to use the slingshot in the first place, everyone offered advice. We were never short on opinions.

"Go for the lock, Jaq. It'll crack open, I know it," I offered.

"No, hit the wood," Zippy said. "It's been on the bottom of the river for years. It'll bust apart"

"No, Scooter's right—hit the lock," Jimmy and Gary said in unison.

Jaq did not answer us. The girl knew what she was doing. Loading another rock into the catch, she pulled back and fired a second shot.

SMACK!

Another direct hit, only this time she hit one of the corners of the chest.

"Hurry, Tommy! She's gonna break the darn thing open," Harrison yelled upward.

Tommy did not answer Harrison because he was in the grip of his own idea. Quickly removing his leather belt, he latched it over the cable, and cinched it tightly around his left hand, which freed up his right hand to reach out for the chest. Inching out, Tommy tested his weight on the cable. Satisfied that the cable latched to the tree limb below would hold his weight, he released his legs and dangled twenty feet above the riverbank.

Jaq took aim and fired again. The shot blew the side of the chest wide open and an old skeleton key dangled from the hole by a small strap of leather.

"There it is!" someone shouted.

Staring upward at the key, Zippy's eyes grew dark like a cartoon character falling in love. At last, his dream was about to be realized. It made me think of how proud his dad would be if he could see his son now.

Tommy looked down and saw Jaq smile as she loaded another rock into the slingshot. This rock was much larger than the first two, so if she connected, it was sure to blow the chest apart. Tommy quickly inched forward, and Jaq pulled back on the sling. He reached out for the chest just as she fired.

The large rock sailed upward in slow motion. It was another perfect shot, but every shot with Jaq was perfect. The girl was like Annie Oakley.

CRACK!

The blast knocked the key into the air and Tommy lunged out as if he was diving for a fly ball. At the last second, he snagged the key, but his weight shifted and the belt slipped. His friends gasped in horror. Tommy was about to fall to his death.

To nobody's surprise, especially mine, Tommy swung his legs up and grabbed the cable. Putting the key in his mouth, he grabbed the other side of his belt and like a zip line in the jungles of Costa Rica, he began his descent towards the fallen tree limb.

I watched in awe because it was a good idea, but what Tommy had not counted on was the steep angle of the cable. He was moving way too fast. At this rate, he would slam right into the fallen tree limb if he did not let go.

True to form, just as he crossed over a sand bar on the riverbank, Tommy released his legs, let go of the belt and landed like a long jumper in a pit of sand.

The impact was so fierce that it knocked the wind out of him. The key popped out of his mouth and landed on his chest. Tommy was not moving. I wondered if he was even breathing. *He's got to be dead,* I thought. We were stunned by what we had just witnessed. However much I disliked him, I did not want to see Tommy Osborne die today. Thoughts of our mortality rushed to the surface of our minds. Sure, we had pushed the envelope here and there, but nobody ever thought one of us would die in the process.

A few seconds passed before Tommy finally moved. Dazed and confused, he sat up and made his way to his feet.

"Get him!" Zippy yelled, tearing after Tommy.

Acting fast, Chris Amato lurched forward and tripped Zippy from behind. He and his brother Joe quickly joined Danny Simon and they raced up the embankment to meet Tommy and Harrison as they grabbed their bikes from the bushes. Tommy held up the key to show us that he was victorious. The gesture dug into me like a red-hot branding iron.

We could only watch as the guys we hated the most peddled away with the key we had worked so hard to find. I felt bad for Zippy. I felt bad for all of us.

"See you later, losers!" Harrison said through his buck teeth as he disappeared into the trees with the others. We could not say anything in return, because right then, we felt as if we had lost. In fact, we had. Tommy had the key and all the glory that went with it. I felt horrible.

TREASURE TIP

If you want to be great,
first you have to think great thoughts.

10

OUR FADED GLORY

News about the discovery traveled fast. Shops were closed, and appointments were put on hold. Filled with anticipation, the people of Port Townsend gathered in front of the Lafitte Public Library. Not everyone was dressed up for Pirates Week, but most people got into the spirit of it. I guess that made it cool, but nothing would make me feel any better.

This year's Pirates Week was about to make history, and Tommy would get all the attention that went with it. I was positive his name would be written in the history books when we got older, and that was eating at me big time.

With the weight of the world on our shoulders, Gary and I pushed our way through the buzzing crowd to join Zippy and Jaq by the fountain. Taking a seat next to Jaq, who was flipping a cootie catcher back and forth, I broke the silence and asked, "Do we know what their prize is?"

"Still waitin' for 'em to come out," she replied.

Zippy's mind must have been going a mile a minute trying to figure out what had gone wrong, because he did not say a word. His shoulders sagged, and his eyes looked at nothing in particular. I knew that look. It was the sullen gaze of defeat.

Seeing this, Gary put his arm around Zippy the way best friends do, but that did not help any. He was down. We all were. Jimmy arrived a few moments later. He did not talk much, either—he was too busy licking the sides of his double-scoop Rocky Road ice cream cone. I wasn't sure how he did it, but Jimmy always managed to find enough time, no matter what was going on, to satisfy the sugar monster living in his stomach.

Looking up, I saw Old Man Sheesley standing with his dog, Koya, across the street. The dog was massive and must have weighed close to 135 pounds. That's a lot of dog, considering I weighed ninety-eight pounds. Koya was different from most Saint Bernards I had seen—not that I had seen a ton of them in town, but this dog was all black with a white chest and face. Some said he was a rare dog because of his coloring, but he was just another dog to me— another really big dog.

A few years ago, there was a rumor going around town that Old Man Sheesley fed Koya the arms and legs of runaway kids. The rumor went something like this: Old Man Sheesley would lure the runaways into his mansion, chop their arms and legs off while they slept and then feed 'em to his dog. That was the reason the white fur around the dog's mouth was stained blood red. I knew it was stupid and just an example of how the rumors in our small town spread like wildfire. I knew it since my dad had told me the dog's mouth was stained red because Old Man Sheesley fed him scraps from Maggie's Butcher Shop over on Water Street.

No matter the time of year or what the weather might be, when Old Man Sheesley was seen, which was not often, he was clothed in a raggedy wool overcoat. His face wore years of loneliness. His long hair was gray and unkempt. The scraggly gray beard made him look like Santa Claus stuck in one of those scary vampire movies. I knew Old Man Sheesley was not a vampire, but he certainly was strange enough to be one. That was weird to even think about—an old man vampire living right here in Port Townsend. I knew vampires were just the stuff of folklore that authors liked to write about. At least I hoped that was the case.

I looked around the crowd, wondering what it would feel like to be the center of all this attention. Everyone I knew, and everyone I didn't know but wanted to know, was there. I'm not sure why I craved attention so much, but I did. Was it my burning desire to fit in and be considered popular? I knew I was not going to figure it out today, so I tried to let go of the thought, but I couldn't. My thoughts were running away from me, and I was feeling the self-pity that comes with defeat. That's the thing about being thirteen years old—the uncertainty of it all. I found that my thoughts would go back and forth between some lie I sold myself on (like I wasn't good enough) and the truth that everything happens for a reason. When I focused on what was true, I immediately felt better about myself.

Just when I was feeling confident and comfortable with myself again, I looked up and saw Brandy Larson walking towards us. *Was she coming to say hello?* I wondered. Then I started to think about the pirate costume I was wearing. Why did I have to be dressed up like a pirate when she was coming to say hi? Did I stink? Was there dirt on my face? I felt my back straighten as she approached, so I stood up and smiled as our eyes met. My heart was beating like the drum line of a marching band.

"Hello Brandy," I said, more self-aware than I had felt all day. The music playing in my head suddenly bucked into a sound like that of a record player needle hitting a scratch on my favorite Elton John album. Her girlfriends, all pretty and more popular than any of us could ever imagine, not to mention perfectly dressed, were now staring directly at me. To my horror, they broke out laughing. Passing us, one of the girls looked at Jaq and laughed even harder.

"Oh my gosh! Did you see what she was wearing?" said the girl with the long, red hair.

"She looks like a boy," another girl quipped as they sauntered off. Turning around, I hoped that Jaq had missed the comments, but she had not. I felt bad for her because the clique of popular girls was really hard on Jaq. As for me, I was humiliated, and if there had been a hole in the cement below my feet, I would have crawled right into it without giving it a second thought. Mortified, I sat down as if I was about to lose a game of musical chairs. My heart was stuck in my throat, and I was completely embarrassed.

Jaq, on the other hand, was amazing as always. She shook off the comment like it was nothing. She was more concerned about me than her own hurt feelings.

"Don't waste your time thinking about that girl, Scott. She's stuck-up and no good."

"Yeah, give it up, man. Brandy Larson is way out of your league," Jimmy said, smacking his lips like a dog eating peanut butter, before he took another lick of his double scoop. I was already feeling down, and I sure did not need a ribbing from Jimmy Finn. When he raised the ice cream cone to his pudgy little face, I knocked his arm just enough to jostle the generous scoops of melting ice cream. In unison, the two scoops fell to the ground, landing with a wet-sounding *THWAP!* Everyone burst out laughing. Everyone but Jimmy.

"What did you do that for?"

"That's what you get!"

"You're gonna pay for that, Scott," Jimmy said tossing his empty cone at me in disgust.

"Yeah, I'd like to see you make me!" I fired back, ready to take on the world. I was back to my thoughts of self-pity and would have been more than happy to take it out on Jimmy, or anyone else for that matter. I was mad. I was mad at the world.

"Knock it off," Gary said, breaking it up.

"He started it, Gary."

"I don't care who started it. Both of you, just knock it off."

"I don't want to be here anymore," Jaq said, tossing her cootie catcher into the trash can. "Let's just go."

"Go where?" I asked, but nobody answered. This was the biggest thing to happen in years, so how could we miss it? But, always thinking, Zippy sat up with his eyes wide as dinner plates. He began to dig into his backpack until a smile crept across his face. "I got an idea," he said, pulling out the water balloon launcher he and his father had made last summer.

"Absolutely!" we all said in unison.

We quickly made our way back through the crowd and onto the sidewalk of Water Street. While most of the stores were closed so everyone could participate in the Pirates

Week hubbub, Jensen's Ice Cream Parlor was still open. Fatman was not one for all the treasure-hunting hoopla, which was why he was still in his shop making ice cream.

Like a team of commandos on a raid, we peered around the corner to see Fatman singing and grooving to the Jackson 5's "ABC," which was playing on his Seeburg Jukebox. That was the great thing about Harley "Fatman" Jensen—he always filled the jukebox with the latest 45s, and his pinball machines were the latest and the greatest. If I hadn't known any better, I would have thought he was a kid trapped in the body of a 300-pound man.

When he turned around to check on the giant ice cream mixer behind the soda counter, we ducked low and ran into the brick-lined alley next to Anderson's Hardware Store. While Fatman allowed us to play our marble games inside the alley, Mr. Anderson, a bitter man in his sixties, often chased us away when the games got too loud, which was more often than not. The reason the games were so competitive was because not only did you get to keep the other guys' marbles when you won, but also, the loser had to spring for a double-scoop chocolate sundae.

After filling Zippy's backpack with water balloons from Anderson's garden hose, we climbed up the fire escape onto Fatman's roof. We found it to be the perfect launching pad for our water balloon assaults on Friday afternoons after school.

We peered over the brick wall of the roof to get a look at our targets.

"Gary, you and Jimmy hold the ends. I'm going first," Zippy said, handing one looped end of the surgical tubing to the guys.

"Oh man, why do you always get to go first?" Jimmy complained.

"Because it was my idea. Plus, I'm a way better shot than you."

"Here they come," I said, probably too loud for the covert mission we were on, but I'd just seen Tommy and his crew being escorted out of the library by Ms. Benson, the librarian. Walking with her was a team of polyester suits—the lawyers representing the Lafitte family estate.

"Shhhhh!" everyone chimed in unison.

"All right ... steady, guys. Here we go!" Zippy said, loading the red water balloon into the sling's tube-sock catch.

"Make sure you don't hit Ms. Benson," I said. "She's got nothing to do with this."

"Yeah, like I'm gonna hit the old librarian. Just relax, Scooter Boy, you're talkin' to Smith & Wesson over here."

Just as Zippy pulled back and let go, Jimmy turned to face him and said, "How—?"

The simple turn of Jimmy's head changed the tension of the tubing, and, as a result, the trajectory of the balloon. It flew off target.

"What are you doing man?" Zippy yelled as we watched the balloon land two streets over to hit the roof of Miller's Automotive.

"I was just sayin' you can't be Smith & Wesson at the same time. They're two guys. You gotta be Smith or you gotta be Wesson. You can't be both," Jimmy said, amused with his retort.

"You're an idiot," Zippy replied, grabbing another balloon.

"What are you kids doing up here?" Somebody's loud booming voice suddenly rocked us from behind.

Spinning around, we all saw Fatman pulling himself off the fire escape ladder. His white apron, spotted with a rainbow of ice cream splatter, stretched across his massive belly. Out of breath, he stalked towards us. We were like a herd of deer, caught in the headlights of trouble.

TREASURE TIP

*Just because you think something,
it does not make it true.*

11

THE SKY IS FALLING

Blocking out the warm sunlight that hoped to reach our fresh young faces, Fatman now stood before us. His knuckles were milky white as his huge hands gripped his massive hips. With his pudgy face looking down at us, more disappointed than I had ever seen him before, his eyes narrowed.

Fear rushed through me like a blown water main. I was confused. Why was he so mad? It's not like we'd stolen something or caused him harm in any way. When I tried to speak up, my mouth stalled in a verbal pause of uncertainty.

"We, we, we … were …," I offered, but my brain was moving like a freight train as it searched for an excuse. I tried to think of something to explain our way out of this one—we had made getting out of trouble into an art form—but this was totally different. Today we were caught red-handed.

"You were what?" he thundered.

"We-we-we …," Gary said, joining in on the brain-burping session of excuses, but he did not know what to say either. Fatman looked down at us, his face contorting with anger like a weird kaleidoscope.

"I'll tell you what you were doing! You were doing it wrong! That's what you were doing," he finally said.

Now, if the looks on our faces could have been translated into speaking terms, we would've sounded like five Scooby Doo's saying in unison, "Zoinks!" We knew Fatman was a cool adult, but no adult was this cool! Not to us, anyway.

"Had ya going, didn't I?" he said as a jolly smile leapt across the folds of his chin.

"Oh man!" Zippy said with a sigh of relief.

"Fatman. Whaddya do that for?" said Gary.

"That's a good one, Fatman," I added.

"You should've seen your faces," Fatman said through a barreling laugh. "Jimmy, my healthy-bellied brother, you'd better check those Fruit of the Looms because you look like you dropped yourself a full load of Rocky Road just now."

When he laughed again, you could see why he was chosen to play Santa Claus for the Christmas parade every year. Sure, he was fat enough, but that jolly laugh of his sealed the deal.

Looking out over Town Square and the crowd that had gathered there, Fatman shook his head in disbelief.

"I hear they beat you to the punch, eh?" he said.

"They stole our thunder, Fatman. That's what they did," Jaq replied, standing next to him.

"I wouldn't let it get to ya. Those Osbornes have been stealin' thunder in this town back to even when I was a kid." Fatman's glance suddenly turned into a distant gaze, as if he was remembering the awkwardness of being the heaviest kid in school and the painful ridicule he'd received at the hands of his classmates, as well as Coach Mike Osborne.

This got me to thinking. Why, as kids, do we make fun of each other so much? Sure, some things are in good fun, and I for one loved a good game of cut-down, but at the end of the day, making someone feel bad about himself was not very nice. I thought about the back and forth I had with Jimmy and how it would always end with some kind of fat joke. The truth was, I had no idea what it was like to be heavy.

"The thing about losing is to make sure the other guys know you haven't given up. It's like striking out in baseball. Right, Scooter?"

"Why do you have to go and say something like that, Fatman? I'm just standing here, minding my own business, and you throw me under the bus like that?"

"That's because when you strike out, you can't feel sorry for yourself. You must dust yourself off and take your medicine. The secret is to be ready next time."

"Next time?" Zippy sprang into the conversation. "There is no next time. It's over and out, Fatman. We lost"

"Then maybe it's time to get even," he said with a smile.

"Well, I don't know if you've noticed or not, but we're not the ones over on the steps of the library claiming the prize," Zippy fired back.

"Well, boo hoo! You just going to sit here and kick rocks for the rest of your life, Zip? Is that it?" Fatman leaned closer to Zippy. "Son, the world gives you lemons—you make ice cream."

"That's not the saying, Fatman," Jimmy replied.

"Who's talkin' here, me or you?" Fatman said, cutting Jimmy off. "Now, you can feel sorry for yourself, or you can keep on truckin'. There's still another key out there somewhere. What makes you think you won't be the ones to find it?"

"Ten years have gone by since Old Man Sheesley found the first key. I ain't got ten years to wait for the next one," Zippy said, looking away in disgust.

"Why you in such a hurry to grow up, little man? You got your entire life ahead of you."

"You ain't the one who got cheated!" Zippy fired back.

"You *ain't*?" Fatman quizzed him.

"Don't start with me, Fatman. I *ain't* in the mood for no English lesson. Not today. Got way too much on my mind."

"Yeah, like focusin' on the big game tonight, and not on what you don't have or what you didn't get," Fatman said.

I knew he was right, but that did not take away the sting of losing.

"You mind if I take a shot?" Fatman asked, breaking the silence that had followed his minilecture. Looking up, I saw that he was already holding a filled water balloon in his giant hands. He was smiling wide like he was thirteen again.

"Yeah, sure," Gary said, smiling back at him. "Zippy, why don't you get the other end? I wanna make sure this one's on target."

"Right. Go ahead and blame me for the miss," Jimmy said defensively.

"Who ya aimin' for, Fatman?" asked Jaq. "Going to hit Tommy?"

"No, little girl. I'm gunnin' for someone my own age," he replied with a mischievous smile.

"Coach Osborne?" we all said, looking at each other.

"I can't let you be the only one to soak that Harbor Master uniform of his," he said with a larger smile.

When Coach Osborne was not coaching his son and the Crab Shack Cardinals, he was the Harbor Master of Port Townsend. That just meant he was in charge of the docks and the ships that came and went. Every Friday, he was one of our favorite targets as he patrolled the parking lot at the docks. To this day he could never figure out where the water balloons were coming from. That's what made Fatman's rooftop the perfect launching pad.

"We've never hit Coach Osborne before," Zippy said, as innocently as he could.

"Then it must be a team of reindeer I keep hearin' on my roof every Friday. Must be their reindeer bikes parked in the alley, too. Now load me up. Let's see if we can bag us an Osborne."

"Okay, Fatman, but you gotta pull it back all the way, then drop to your knees before you let go," Zippy said, giving instructions.

"You think you're the first to make a water balloon launcher there, Zippy? They used to call me Sure Shot Smith & Wesson," Fatman said, loading the balloon into the catch. Before Jimmy could chime in again about Smith & Wesson being two different people, Fatman barked out his orders.

"Jaq, you and Scooter get behind Gary and Zippy."

"What should I do, Fatman?" Jimmy asked, feeling left out.

"Watch and learn," Zippy quickly answered as Fatman stretched the launcher farther than I had ever seen it stretched.

He closed one eye and took aim at Coach Osborne, who was smiling on the steps of the library with his arm around Tommy. Ms. Benson stood next to them, addressing the crowd. No doubt she was describing the latest discovery and revealing the contents of the third safe-deposit box. Fatman released a deep breath and let go of the giant slingshot.

As the balloon took flight, it began to contort back and forth like a jellyfish swimming through the ocean. When the crowd began to applaud the announcement of the prize, Coach Osborne looked up just in time to see the water balloon hit him dead square in the chest. He was soaked. It was a perfect shot. As we started to celebrate the accomplishment, Fatman quickly ordered us to duck down out of sight, but it was too late. Coach Osborne looked right into my eyes.

"Run!" Fatman yelled, crouching low as he ran to the fire escape. I was amazed at how fast the big man could move. You would never guess he weighed 300 pounds the way he flew down that fire escape like a firefighter answering the bell of a four-alarm fire. Trouble was coming our way and we needed to run faster than we had ever run before.

TREASURE TIP

If you don't have anything nice to say,
don't say anything at all.

12

BUSTED

I landed upright in the dirt-filled alley and saw Fatman upending his aluminum trash cans, one after the other. With his massive Big Foot-like feet, he began to kick the garbage in every direction.

"What are you doing?" I asked.

"We gotta get outta here!" Gary said, moving towards Water Street.

"There's no time," Fatman said, out of breath from his rapid descent from the roof. "Running only makes you look guilty."

"But we *are* guilty," Jimmy said.

"Yeah, we gotta go, Fatman!" Zippy shouted.

"No! No! No! We can hide," Jaq said, but Fatman would not be denied.

"Everybody, just calm down. If you follow my lead, I'll get you kids out of this."

There was a quick moment of indecision: Fight or flight? Running had served us so well in the past it was hard to think about sticking around to actually face our accusers. The sounds of feet pounding on the pavement of Water Street left us with no decision.

"Now, here they come," said Fatman. "You all just start pickin' up the trash and let me do the talking."

Coach Osborne, followed by Tommy and his crew, appeared at the end of the alley. We were trapped. Coach Osborne was fuming; his Harbor Master uniform was soaked like a wet kitchen sponge.

"I saw you, Scott Martin," he said with disdain. "I saw you up on that rooftop."

"Huh?" I said, picking up a piece of trash covered in melted ice cream.

"Why, Mike, you been playin' in the sprinklers again?" Fatman said, cutting him off. "Look at you, you're all wet."

"Shut up, Fat Boy! I'm talkin' to these little delinquents."

Coach Osborne sounded like an angry school principal. I could see why he was perfect for his job as Harbor Master of Port Townsend. He had the attitude of a bully and the bulky body to back it up.

"You're dead meat, Martin," Tommy said to me.

Like father, like son, I thought. Before I could respond, Jimmy's dad rolled up in his police cruiser. Coach Osborne quickly spun around as Sheriff Dale Finn climbed from his car. Unlike Jimmy, who was pudgy and somewhat awkward, Sheriff Finn had a large athletic build. The keys on his gun belt jingled as he stepped forward like a gunfighter from the Wild West.

"You going to do something this time?" Coach Osborne fired off. "I told you these juvenile delinquents were the ones throwing those water balloons."

"I take it you're the one who got hit?" Sheriff Finn said, stating the obvious.

"Wow, Dale! Whatever gave you that idea?"

When Sheriff Finn looked up to the roof, down the alley and across the street into the Town Square, Fatman joined in.

"That's an awfully long throw for a kid, Mike," Fatman said with a smile. "Not even you could throw a water balloon that far."

"I told you, Fat Boy, keep your big nose out of this."

"Or what? You gonna beat me up after recess?"

"All right, that's enough," Sheriff Finn said, trying to get control of the situation.

"Are you going to search their backpacks?"

"Mike, I don't have any right to search anyone's backpacks, including yours," Sheriff Finn replied.

"I don't have a backpack filled with water balloons. They do!"

"If you did—"

"That's your own son, for cryin' out loud."

"Yeah, and he's got rights here just like everybody else."

Coach Osborne's eyes narrowed. He stepped closer to Sheriff Finn. "I can't wait for your re-election."

"That makes two of us," Sheriff Finn replied.

I could see the veins on Coach Osborne's neck bulging with anger. I wanted to laugh, but I knew that probably would not go over too well.

"Come on, boys, let's go see our new boat," he said.

As they walked out of the alley, Tommy glared back at me. I opened my eyes wider, taunting him as if to say, *'Bring it on, Chump!'* I guess my new revelation of being nice to others had not lasted very long, but this was Tommy, so I did not feel like I had gone back on the promise.

"Does that mean we can count you out for hangin' re-election posters, Mike?" Fatman said with a laugh.

Coach Osborne did not laugh. He did not look back either.

"So, that's their prize? A boat?" I asked Sheriff Finn.

"Seems like it."

"Mind if we go check it out?" Gary asked.

Sheriff Finn did not answer Gary's question. He simply looked us over, glanced at his son Jimmy and finally gazed at Fatman, who nodded his opinion that Sheriff Finn should let us go.

"If you agree this'll be the last time I hear of a balloon launch from a rooftop."

We all nodded in agreement.

"What about from sidewalks?" Zippy asked.

"What do you say we get through the summer and talk about sidewalks next year?"

"Fair enough, Sheriff. Fair enough," Zippy replied. "Come on, guys. Let's go check out this boat."

"You have a game in two hours," Sheriff Finn reminded us. "Try not to get into any more trouble."

"Yes sir!" we agreed again.

"And Jimmy?" Sheriff Finn turned to his son. Fearing some kind of grounding, or worse, Jimmy's eyes squinted before rising to meet his father's. "Your mother wants you to do your chores before you head to the ballpark, so no dilly-dallying down at the docks."

"Yes sir," Jimmy said, excited by having just dodged trouble with his dad.

As we exited the alley, Sheriff Finn turned his attention back to Fatman, who was re-tying his apron, which had come loose during the scattering.

I decided to hold back and listen to their conversation.

"You know, you covering for them like this—" Sheriff Finn started to say.

"Who said I was covering for 'em, Dale?"

"Well, that's just great, Harley. You're going to get it into their minds that they can do whatever they want, and that's just not a good thing."

"Take it easy, Dale. They're thirteen years old. Nothing wrong with a little fun now and again."

"Not at someone else's expense, no matter who it is. I'm just sayin ..."

"And I'm just sayin' it felt good to finally strike back against that guy."

"You're the one who hit Mike with the water balloon?" Sheriff Finn inquired, but Fatman simply smiled without admitting anything.

"Still fightin' back the old age, eh Harley?" Sheriff Finn said with a smile. "You're going to have to grow old sometime."

"You don't stop laughin' when you grow old, Dale. You grow old when you stop laughin'."

"I'll keep that in mind."

"Ah, Mike's been a bully since you and I were kids, and that boy of his is no different. He makes fun of your kid and threatens just about anyone who stands up to him."

Sheriff Finn took in the information he already knew. Looking up at Fatman, he asked, "You want a ride down to the docks, see what this boat looks like?"

"Do I look like the kind of guy who goes boating?"

"Come on, already! Let's go, Scooter!" the guys yelled from the end of the street.

I smiled at Sheriff Finn as he climbed into his cruiser because I was glad Jimmy had a dad like him. He was strict and he was a police officer, but every so often the man showed signs of coolness. He was not bad as far as adults go.

We made quick work of the six blocks down to the marina, but when we arrived, it was anything but a celebration for Tommy's prize. There was no fanfare for something amazing—just a departing crowd. Some people were even laughing. If I hadn't seen it with my own eyes, I never would have believed it.

TREASURE TIP

Every moment is another adventure waiting to happen.

13

AN EMPTYVESSEL

L
ike a school of salmon swimming upstream to spawn, we pushed through the departing crowd to find Coach Osborne standing on the deck of a very large sailboat. Tommy, the Amato Twins, Harrison and Danny Simon could be seen through the portal windows, frantically searching for anything of value.

Coach Osborne was busy arguing with Tommy about continuing to search for treasure on what looked like a hunk of junk. We were captivated by their argument until we noticed that the rest of the crowd had left. Sharing quick looks back and forth, we scattered as if a game of hide-and-seek had suddenly broken out. Though we had taken off in different directions, we ended up huddled together behind the wooden railings of a nearby houseboat. From our vantage point, Coach Osborne was right. The third prize of the *Keys of Lafitte* treasure hunt was nothing more than a broken-down sailboat, some fifty feet long. With its faded teakwood, and the lines running frayed and worn up to the mast, the old vessel was a floating shipwreck.

Tommy and his friends finally emerged from inside the boat, sweaty and ruffled from what had obviously been an exhaustive search. They were defeated and dejected.

"That's it?" Zippy whispered with a smirk. "What a hunk of junk!"

Before anyone could chime in, Gary quickly ordered us to get down, as Coach Osborne began to turn in our direction. He had not heard Zippy's laugh; he was simply ordering the boys off the boat. Disappointed, they left the boat one by one and headed to the parking lot. Gary expertly mirrored their movements, hiding between the adjoining boats along the way, to make sure they were indeed leaving. I thought it was funny that Tommy and his friends had been on top of the world just thirty minutes ago, and now they were down in the dumps. I did not feel sorry for them, because when word got out the treasure was a decaying sailboat worth more as salvage than anything else, ridicule would soon follow. Yep, they deserved all the attention that was coming to them.

"All right, the coast is clear," Gary said, returning from his lookout.

We moved in for a closer look. Wiping away the grime from the porthole windows, we peered inside the old sailboat. It was a mess and, much like the exterior, junked and gutted. The cushions had been ripped open and all the stuffing was torn out, no doubt compliments of Coach Osborne's anxious pocketknife. The cabinet doors were open, but there was nothing inside. Tommy and his gang had searched the boat and found nothing—not a single gold coin or silver Piece of Eight.

How could this be? I thought. How could the great Jacques Pierre Lafitte plan on giving away this pile of junk as the prize for his great-grandfather's lost treasure hunt?

It did not make sense. There had to be an explanation. Perhaps the boat had been new forty years ago when he got the idea for the treasure hunt, but from the looks of it, I could not imagine this boat ever being new. I was at a loss, and I was not alone.

"I don't get it," Gary said, scratching his head.

"Kind of feels like we're missing something, doesn't it?" Jaq added. "This old junker is the prize?"

"Or maybe it's not supposed to be a prize at all," Zippy said with a breath of enthusiasm. "My father said when Old Man Sheesley took over the Lafitte mansion, it was a dump too, but you don't see him complaining."

"So ...," I said with my face still pressed against the porthole window.

"So maybe we have to look at this not like a dead end, but just another piece of the puzzle," Zippy continued.

"Okay, smarty pants, where's this old junker fit into this *puzzle* of yours?" Jimmy asked, making imaginary quotes in the air. "You heard Tommy's dad. They didn't find anything."

"Maybe because they were looking for a stash of gold or silver."

"Well, yeah. Duh!"

"What do you mean, Zip?" Gary asked, stepping closer.

"I don't know … maybe they should've been searching for the metaphor."

"The meta-what?"

"Jimmy, do you ever pay attention in class?" Zippy said, looking around the boat as he talked. "A metaphor compares two things without using the words *like* or *as*."

"Like this treasure hunting is a big fat waste of time?"

"No, Jimmy, like *Jaq is a speeding bullet when she runs*. That's a metaphor, and I'm telling you each key in this hunt has got to be some kind of metaphor for the next one."

"Sounds good, Zip, but the last one was a house," I added.

"Yes, and before that, a horse-drawn carriage."

"So what's all that have to do with a boat?"

"You guys are killin' me. I don't have all the answers here. I'm just saying."

"Yeah, well I'm just sayin' it doesn't make sense," Jimmy quickly added.

"Man, what is your problem?" Zippy shot back. "Of course it doesn't make sense right now. Creation. Discovery. These things take time."

While the debate continued back and forth as always, I peered through the porthole window again, but this time I saw something different. Directly above a section of the cabinets, I saw a small infinity symbol carved into the teakwood.

My mind ignited with possibilities, but before I could make sense out of what I was looking at, an adult voice suddenly shot up in the distance.

"Hey, you kids!" the voice bellowed. "Get off that boat!"

Nobody knew where the voice was coming from, because when trouble closed in on us, we ran like the wind. We bolted down the docks and made our way up the gangway to the parking lot. It was another clean escape. Out of breath and laughing from what we had just experienced, we began to talk about our baseball game, which was only an hour away. We had to hurry home, change into our uniforms and be at the ballpark for warm-ups in twenty-five minutes.

With all the commotion, I forgot to tell anyone about what I saw, but it was not to be the last time I saw the infinity symbol that day. In a few short hours, everything would change.

TREASURE TIP

Sometimes a dead-end is really a new beginning.

14

PLAY BALL

Fresh cut grass, grilling hot dogs, and roasted heaps of peanuts mixed into the warm summer air. For me, this was what summer smelled like, especially at Pacheco Park, the baseball field on the north side of town. The electronic scoreboard in left field read: Crab Shack Cardinals 1, Jensen's Ice Cream 0. We were losing.

The first eight innings of the game had raced by without incident as the game turned into a pitching duel between Zippy and Tommy. The radio announcer calling the game was Skip Johnson. He attended Brown University, which was like a million miles away in Providence, Rhode Island,

and spent his summers here with his mother, Millie Johnson, a long time resident of Port Townsend.

While walking from the dugout, I saw Skip stand up inside the green press box behind home plate. He was razor thin and wore these round eyeglasses. He looked like Frank Sinatra, the way he held the mic as he set the stage.

"Here we are in the bottom of the ninth, with two outs and Jensen's Ice Cream trailing by one run in the city league championship series. These ice cream kids, the scrappiest team in the Jefferson County League, have an amazing one-game lead over the defending champions, the Crab Shack Cardinals. Any hope for a win tonight rests on the small shoulders of little Scott 'My Favorite' Martin. But that's Tommy 'Lights Out' Osborne on the mound, and the kid hasn't lost a game all season. From the looks of his pitching tonight, I'd say he's about to record his fifth shutout of the season."

I looked over at the announcer and wanted to say something sarcastic about the "My Favorite Martian" television show reference, but my eyes caught the wavy blonde hair of Brandy Larson, who was in the stands right behind home plate. When Brandy smiled, I practically tripped over my own baseball cleats as I stepped into the batter's box. I heard a trickle of laughter from the infield, but I quickly caught my balance and acted as if I was stretching out my hamstrings. Sneaking a quick glance towards her, I realized she was not smiling at me at all. She was smiling at Tommy, who was staring me down from the pitcher's mound.

I looked over to first base where Zippy was standing after a rare single up the middle. "Come on, Scooter. His arm's tired. Lay off the high stuff and let him walk ya."

Walk me? I thought to myself. My whole season has come down to this moment. I was not about to take a walk. This was a moment of opportunity. I wanted to seize it because a home run would win the ballgame for us; and for a guy who batted ninth in the order, a home run would finally crown me as MVP of the series.

Stepping into the batter's box, I felt my heart pound so hard that it started to shake my eyeballs. This was a bad thing for a batter. You never want to step into the batter's box with shaking eyeballs. If I did not calm down, there was no way I would ever hit Tommy's fastball. A few deep breaths were followed by my right hand raised towards the umpire to let him know I was not ready. Reggie Jackson, my favorite major league player of all, did this every time he stepped into the batter's box. Over the season, it had become my trademark. Everybody needed a trademark, and this was mine, thanks to Reggie Jackson.

Digging my cleats into the dirt surrounding home plate, I planted each foot securely with growing determination. A few practice swings back and forth, and I was finally ready. When I looked up to find Tommy smiling at me from the pitcher's mound, I felt my heart jump into my throat, so I stepped out of the batter's box to gather my thoughts.

"Come on, man. Let's go already!" someone yelled from the outfield.

I turned and looked back at the dugout to find Jimmy and the rest of my teammates with their faces pressed up against the fence. Everyone was offering me the obvious advice for hitting a baseball: Keep your eye on the ball! Head down! Swing all the way through! Things like that, which I already knew.

Just as I was about to step back into the batter's box, Gary yelled at me from the on-deck circle. "Lay off that high fast ball, Bro. You know he's going to throw it."

Gary then placed his right index finger to his temple. This was his way of telling me to be a smart batter. It was something our father always did whenever we messed up at home, but I knew Gary was just hoping I could get a base hit so he could have his chance at the plate. He was our leadoff batter, our best batter, but this was my moment. This was my moment to shine.

"A walk is as good as a hit!" someone yelled from the stands.

"Don't listen to 'em, Scott!" Jaq yelled. "Hit the cover off that ball!"

Jaq always sat next to my mom and dad because her dad was not a baseball fan. I smiled and nodded at her as I stepped into the box. *This is what it's all about,* I said to myself. *This is what champions are made of.*

"*Playyyyy* ball!" the umpire shouted over me.

I checked my batting glove, swung the bat up onto my shoulder, and focused on the ball in Tommy's hand. He smiled again, checked Zippy at first base, and then went into his wind up.

"Hey batter, batter, batter, batter!" the infield chattered.

It was like time was standing still before me. Things were moving in slow motion. Everything, that is, except the ball leaving Tommy's outstretched hand. Before I knew what had happened, I heard the umpire yell, "*Steeeeerike* one!"

I'm not sure I even saw the ball leave Tommy's hand as my bat swung through the air. Looking back, I saw the catcher standing to catch the high fastball. He offered a slight chuckle.

"Like taking candy from a baby," he said as he threw the ball back to Tommy. I had blown it. I had swung at the high fastball, which everyone warned me about, but I did not care. Somewhere deep inside, I knew I could hit the pitch.

"Come on, Scott. Lay off that junk!" Gary yelled as he slammed his bat into the ground. "Be smart up there."

"That's all right, son!" my dad offered from the stands with his hands cupped around his mouth like a megaphone. "You can do it, just keep your head down and make a level swing."

"Just like Reggie Jackson, sweetie," Mom said, clapping her hands together, which shook her beehive hairdo back and forth like something you'd see on a Saturday morning cartoon.

Jaq stood up next to her. "You can do it, Scott. You can hit this guy."

I dug my cleats back into the dirt of the batter's box and raised the bat to my shoulder again. This time I would be ready.

Keep your eye on the ball and give it a ride, I thought, silently coaching myself.

"Hey batter, batter, batter, batter ..."

Tommy wasted no time, and before I knew it, I heard a *SLAP!* when the ball hit the catcher's mitt a second time. I froze, waiting for the inevitable judgment from the umpire standing behind me.

"Ball!" the umpire said, less enthusiastically than his call for a strike.

"Thatta boy!" I heard my dad yell amongst the cheering fans. It was at this moment that I heard an angry voice shoot from the dugout of the Cardinals, which nobody could miss.

"You walk this kid and I'll put your butt on the bench!" Coach Osborne yelled at his son. When he felt the eyes from the disapproving crowd descend upon him, Coach Osborne snapped a nasty glare right back at them. "What are you looking at?" he said to one of the men in the stands.

The man simply shook his head in amazement before looking away. I felt sorry for Tommy. It was just for a second, but nobody deserved that kind of treatment from a parent, not even Tommy. He dug the ball into his glove with fire in his eyes. He was determined to strike me out. He was mad, and I knew he was going to bring the fastball, so I got ready.

"*Steeeeerike* two!" the umpire yelled even louder as my bat whiffed through the summer air a second time.

Like the first time, I was not even close. The pitch was another high fastball, but not as high as the first strike. Now the count was one ball and two strikes. I was behind in the count, or as they say on television, I was "in the hole."

At this point, I was not listening to my dugout, because I knew they were mad. In fact, I was so focused I could not hear anything at all. I just saw their angry faces offering more advice. I knew I had been told more than once about Tommy's high fastball, something he knew I loved to swing at, but again, I knew I could hit the pitch. I dug back into the batter's box. I would be ready this time, because I suddenly had a great idea. Instead of crouching down in a traditional batter's stance, I decided to stand more upright. This way I would be at the same level as the high fastball. I was happy with my decision, so I dug my cleats in and raised my bat.

Tommy checked on Zippy at first base and went into his wind up. I saw the ball leave his hand this time. It was another high fastball, but something was happening to the pitch. It was an off-speed pitch. *Oh no!* I quickly said to myself. Tommy had tricked me. It was not a fastball. It was a sinkerball. Now, the sinkerball is an ugly pitch and almost impossible to hit. They called it a sinkerball because at the very last second, the bottom falls out of the pitch and "sinks" into the strike zone.

Swing! I yelled to myself. *You have to swing!*

With my mind racing, I quickly changed the trajectory of my swing to anticipate the sinker, but the bottom of the pitch fell out so far I knew my swing was going to be too high.

Oh nooooooo! I yelled to myself as I felt the bat swing past the ball, which slapped into the worn leather of the catcher's mitt with a resounding echo in my mind.

"*Steeeeerike* three! You're out!" the umpire yelled. I could hear Skip's voice raving about the amazing pitch by "this talented thirteen-year-old Little Leaguer."

The game was over and we had lost. The championship series was now tied at one game apiece. I knew it was my fault that we had lost, but I did not want to hear it. In fact, I did not want to hear anything at that moment. I just wanted to go home, so I kept my eyes low as I slapped hands with the enemy before returning to the dugout. I knew Tommy was laughing at me with his teammates, who were rushing the mound to celebrate. I would not look over and give them the satisfaction of ridiculing me. Not this time. Not any time, for that matter.

Entering the dugout, I felt the comforting hand of Coach Palmer on my shoulder. He was a firefighter in town and the father of our center fielder, Phillip Palmer. He was a good coach, and he always had great things to say to us, but nothing could change the fact that I had just struck out.

After waiting for the crowd to disperse, I walked out to join my brother, who was no doubt talking to our parents about my last at-bat. He was probably saying how I should have done this, or should have done that. All he really cared about was having his last at bat and perhaps winning the game for us. I could not blame him. He was one of those guys who, whenever the game was on the line, wanted the ball. He thrived on pressure. Me? Not so much.

After walking through a crowd of teammates and their families, who said nothing to me or about me, I looked up to see Brandy Larson, Tommy and their friends walking right towards me in celebration. I did an about-face like I was some kind of trained soldier in the Army. The problem with executing an about-face so quickly is you do not have time to see where you're going. As a result, I ran right into Old Man Sheesley and bounced off him like a small running back hitting a 375-pound defensive lineman.

Falling to the ground, I reached out for anything to regain my balance. Unfortunately for me, that thing was the cup of soda in Old Man Sheesley's aging hands. The cold soda drenched my uniform.

"Smooth move, Ex-Lax," Tommy said to a chorus of laughter as he walked past with the others.

Looking up, I saw Old Man Sheesley staring down at me. I froze, not because I was embarrassed, but because the lights of the baseball park bounced off of a silver pendant hanging around his neck. I blinked a few times, trying to make out his face, which I was certain to be filled with anger, but the pendant hanging around his neck caught my focus. It was the same infinity symbol I had seen carved into the teakwood of Tommy's shipwrecked sailboat.

Old Man Sheesley simply grunted and kept on walking. In the blink of an eye, my embarrassment for the entire night cleared like the morning fog lifting into the afternoon sun. At that moment I saw everything clearly and knew everything *did* happen for a reason. If I had not struck out, I would not have walked out of the dugout in fear of ridicule from others, and I would not have bumped into Old Man Sheesley. If I had not bumped into Old Man Sheesley, I would not have seen the pendant dangling at the end of his necklace.

I guess sometimes you have to go down an undesirable path to get to what you want in life, which made me think of what Fatman said: "You got to keep on truckin' when times get tough, because they shape who you are to become."

I wanted to ask Old Man Sheesley for a closer look or the meaning of his pendant, but by the time I got to my feet, I had lost him in the departing crowd. There was no time to explain to the others what had just happened. I knew I had to get to the sailboat before Tommy and his teammates did, so I jumped on my bike and rode for the marina as fast as I could.

TREASURE TIP

Believe in your abilities,
not your dis-abilities.

15

DON'T STOP BELIEVING

L iving in the Pacific Northwest had many advantages during the summer, but the coolest advantage was that it was now close to seven o'clock and the sun would not go down for another two hours. The long days of summer gave us more time to play before the streetlights came on, which signaled our curfew to go inside for the night.

Using every shortcut I knew, I made it to the marina lickety-split. I'm guessing it must have taken me seven minutes at best. Stashing my bike behind the dumpsters in the parking lot, I noticed the boats of the marina gently rocking back and forth from the rising tide, indicating the day's slow transition into night. My heart began to pound with anticipation for what lay before me.

Checking my surroundings, I quietly pulled myself up onto the locked gate leading to the docks. Just as I was about to swing my leg over, the gate swung open from the momentum of my upward jump. *Never assume anything,* I thought. I should have checked to see if the gate was locked before I climbed up it like a monkey. So there I was, straddling the metal gate as it swung back and forth like some kind of amusement park ride. A seagull sitting on a nearby post squawked as if to laugh at my predicament. I quickly swung my leg over and jumped to the docks below.

Making my way to Tommy's sailboat, which barely rocked from my weight, I quietly slid back the galley door. The musty air wafted upward from the boat's interior. Closing the door behind me, I could not help but wonder if I was climbing into the last remaining pirate ship ever to sail these waters. I wondered if any pirates had ever walked the plank on this boat. Walking the plank must have been a horrible way to die, as if there could be a good way.

Daydreaming about the boat's history, I found myself looking at nothing in particular. It was just one of those stares where you get lost in your thoughts, but I was not thinking about anything. I was allowing my imagination to run wild. Pirates? Walking the plank? I uttered a nervous laugh as I reminded myself that I was okay and Jean Lafitte was not going to make me walk the plank, although that would have been kind of a cool way to meet him.

Just as I began to move my feet towards the carved infinity symbol in the teakwood before me, a strange sound sprang up from the darkness. I froze. What the heck was that? Was someone inside the boat with me? Maybe it was Jean Lafitte's ghost, here to protect his treasure.

I laughed again because I knew my mind was playing tricks on me. But when I heard the sound again, I spun around to find two eyes glowing in the dark crawl space. My heart raced. My mouth was suddenly as dry as a sandbox. What the heck was I looking at?

There was something odd about the eyes staring at me from the darkness. They were not as large as I had initially thought, so I strained to focus in the dim light and discovered that the eyes belonged to a small rat, which at this moment was busy chewing on the plastic coating of some exposed wires from the control panel.

"Hey little guy," I said as if I was talking to a baby. "Are you eating some plastic for dinner?" The rat opened his mouth and hissed like a ferocious tiger. I would like to say that I did not react in fear of such a small, seemingly harmless creature, but before I knew what had happened, I was on my butt when my baseball cleats snagged on the foam stuffing of the cushions under my feet.

I grabbed the nearest pillow and fired it at the rat in retaliation. He scurried back into the darkness as I pulled myself back to a standing position. Why the heck was I ending up on my butt so much today? I did not wait to answer my own question. I simply turned my attention to the task at hand and stood in front of the carved infinity symbol.

With close inspection, I saw that the symbol was a perfect match to the symbol hanging around Old Man Sheesley's neck. I ran my fingers across it, wondering what secrets it held. Why was it here on this boat, and why was it carved into the teakwood panel? Was there a hidden compartment?

"Yes," I whispered. "That had to be it."

Searching for a latch, or some type of release, I ran my hand across the surface of the teakwood paneling, but found nothing. Maybe I was wrong. Maybe this was just some sort of Lafitte family crest we knew nothing about.

Momentarily defeated, I stared at the carved symbol while I asked myself, *What would Zippy do?* I said this because Zippy had a way of thinking things through more logically than the rest of us. For me, I ran my life with my emotions on my sleeve, which sometimes got me in trouble, but thinking about Zippy seemed to help me work things out when I faced a mental roadblock like the one before me.

I knew Zippy would start from the beginning and work his way up to the current problem, which seemed logical, but I did not have time for that. I knew Tommy would be arriving with the others any second, so I had to think fast, and move even faster.

Maybe there were other symbols in the boat, and together, they would form some kind of triangulation to "X marks the spot," like down at the river. After scanning the interior of the cabin, I discovered that this was the only visible symbol. At this moment, something occurred to me. What if the symbol was the "X," and the prize—or whatever I was to find—was somehow hidden behind it?

With no other options running through my mind, I quickly removed the shelves the cabinet next to the symbol and got to work. I tapped on the wood inside of the cabinet. The top. The bottom. The back. The sides.

Tap! Tap! Tap! Thunk!

"What was that?" I said out loud, as if Gary and the others were with me, but they were not. There was just the rat hiding in the darkness—and me.

Tap! Tap! Tap! Thunk!

I had found a hollowed-out section of the cabinet! A pry bar! I would need something to pry open the side of the cabinet. I felt around the piles of junk left behind by the initial search of the boat, found an old butter knife in a drawer and wondered if the knife itself was worth something. It looked old and perhaps made of silver, but I knew time was of the essence, so I jammed the blade into the seam of the old wood. As I pried the small piece of wood open, the silver knife began to bend under the stress.

CRACK!

Just as the knife was about to bend back onto itself, the piece of wood splintered out and broke off. The years at sea and damp weather conditions of the Pacific Northwest had rotted much of the boat's interior, including the hard teakwood.

The hole in the wood was just big enough to slip my small hand through. Reaching inside, all the way up to my armpit, I felt my way through the dark, damp hole to the backside of the teakwood panel where the symbol was. And there, I felt something. It was a long cylinder, about the size of an aluminum cigar holder like the kind Gary and I would save dimes in when Dad smoked a cigar on "special occasions." His special occasions, however, had since moved to the open water of the sea, because Mom hated the smell of burning tobacco since her father had died of emphysema. Emphysema was a deadly lung disease, and ever since Grandpa's passing, our mom would not have any smoking in the house. She was so concerned that Gary and I might experiment with cigarettes, she made a sign and posted it on the refrigerator for everyone to see, including Dad: *1250 people die from smoking every ... single ... day.*

Getting back to work, I grabbed the cylinder and pulled, but it would not budge because I could not get a good grip on it. Maybe it was just part of the boat's electrical system, but why was it right behind the symbol? From what I could tell, all the electronics were on the other side of the cabin, so whatever it was, it appeared to be out of place.

Pulling my hand out, I grabbed the knife and tried to use it as a pry bar inside the dark, musty hole. Using the flat end of the knife, I carefully slipped the blade behind the cylinder and began to pry it from the wood. Suddenly, I felt something move. I had to be careful not to pry the cylinder all the way off without holding it with one finger. Who knew where it would land inside the dark cubbyhole of the cabinetry. *If I could just get my other hand in there,* I thought, but there was no room for that, so I kept prying with the knife while wrapping one finger around the cylinder just in case it popped free.

Suddenly, I heard voices coming down the gangway. I strained to listen and quickly recognized Tommy's voice mixed in with the others. I had to hurry. Prying harder with the knife, I felt the cylinder finally break free. It slipped from my hand. I dropped the knife and jammed my arm into the dark abyss. It felt like my arm was in the jaws of a bear trap, the way the splintered wood around the hole chewed into my skin.

TREASURE TIP

Your imagination can lift you up or down. It's up to you.

16

THE CADDY

Just as the mysterious metal cylinder brushed past my
index finger on its rapid descent into the unknown
darkness of the floating shipwreck, my palm snapped
shut like G.I. Joe's Kung Fu Grip. Between my little pinky
finger and the base of my palm, I held the mysterious
cylinder with all the strength I could muster.

Pulling the cylinder from the jagged hole of the
cupboards, I made my way to the front cabin of the boat.
I could hear their voices right outside. Then, slowly, the
galley door slid open. I ducked to the side of the small

space I was now in and saw small slivers of sunlight cutting through the darkness like razor blades. Gazing upward, I found my path to freedom. The front hatch of the boat was directly over my head. Freedom was mine. But I was not free. I was anything but free.

Reaching up, I quickly spun the knobs that held the hatch in place. The problem I faced, however, was the rusted knobs of the hatch. With every other turn, the old metal knobs squeaked like a hysterical mouse caught in a trap.

"What was that?" I heard Tommy ask the others. "I heard something."

My fingers froze on the knobs. I would have to wait for one of them to speak before I could execute another turn. With each turn I was closer to freedom.

"It's an old boat, man," Joe Amato said. "It's full of noises."

Twist. Squeak. Twist. Squeak.

"Yeah, full of noises, but no treasure?" Danny quipped.

"Yeah, what a gyp," Chris Amato agreed.

"What's that?" someone asked.

"What?" Tommy asked.

"That hole in the cupboard," Danny replied. "That wasn't here a few hours ago."

I could hear their movements near the evidence of my discovery. I had to move fast. Using their chattering conversation as cover, I spun the knobs and slowly swung the hatch open. To my horror, this resulted in an even louder creaking sound from the rusty hinges of the hatch.

"Did you hear that?" Tommy announced. His voice was moving towards me.

It was now or never. I had to make a run for it. I knew if I could make it to my bike, I could out-pedal them for sure. Nobody could catch me when I was on the Schwinn Stingray, especially off-road where my knobby tires would hold the faster speeds I loved so much.

Just as Tommy entered the front cabin, I pulled myself onto the bow of the boat. I looked down at him as he peered up at me through the open hatch.

"See you around, loser!" I said with a smile, which quickly evaporated like water on the hot sidewalk of a summer day. Tommy's face twisted in so much anger I did not know what to do, so I slammed the hatch shut.

"Get him!" I heard him shout to the others.

Moving fast, I jumped off the boat and cleared the bow-lines like a runaway jackrabbit in a single leap. I was in full stride by the time they scrambled out of the galley and onto the stern of the massive boat. The chase was on.

Running through the gate at the end of the docks, I reached my bike, swung my leg over and took off. Tommy and his crew were right behind me, pedaling fast.

With my feet like the turning pistons of a turbo-charged Mustang Fastback, I rode up Baker Hill and turned onto Sunnyside Avenue. I could hear Tommy and the others riding up behind me, but I still had a good lead on them.

Heading back towards Pacheco Park, I made a quick turn onto Water Street, pushing my tires to the limit. Rounding the corner, I figured I could lose them in the alleys behind the shops of Water Street.

"There he is!" I heard Jaq yell as I approached.

She was with Gary, Zippy and Jimmy, eating ice cream outside of Jensen's Ice Cream Shop. Fatman was sitting at the table next to them, enjoying the calmness of night, which was shattered by my arrival.

"Where are you going?" Gary yelled as I rode past them like a wild man.

"Meet me at the Caddy!" I screamed back as I kept my feet on the pedals, wishing I had a set of gears, because I was spinning out the single gear of my Schwinn. All they could do was watch as Tommy and his thugs rode past, gaining on me with every pedal stroke.

"We should go help him," I heard Jimmy say.

"Nah, he'll be fine."

"Yeah, he'll lose them on Franklin Street without a doubt," Zippy said.

"Meet him at the Caddy is what he said, and that's what we're going to do," Gary added, climbing to his feet.

"The Caddy?" Fatman asked.

"Sorry, Fatman. It wouldn't be a hideout if we told you," Zippy answered as he began to pedal away.

"You know Chevy hates people on his lot after closin' time."

"What makes you think we're going to Hergenrader's junkyard?" Jimmy asked.

"Because Chevy's had that ol' Caddy along the back fence since I was in school," Fatman said with a smile. "I told you. There isn't much I haven't done in this town. I know all."

"Yeah, Fatman. We'll see ya!" Jaq said as she climbed onto her bike.

"Wouldn't wanna be ya!" Jimmy fired back with a laugh.

Fatman leaned back on his chair, creaking from the mere girth of his body, and ended his day as he always did, sitting in front of his shop, watching the world pass by and the sun drift behind the distant mountains.

Helmut "Chevy" Hergenrader was from Germany and looked much older than his fifty years. He had one leg and claimed to have lost the other in World War II, but everyone in town knew that was just the story he told. I thought he looked more like Long John Silver the way he hobbled around the junkyard on that wooden leg of his, but his nickname, Chevy, was set in stone. You would not dare call him Chevy to his face, however. In fact, you'd have to be crazy to get in his face about much of anything.

The rumor around town was he had lost his leg back when my dad was a kid. The Chevy he was working on suddenly fell off the jack and crushed his right leg beyond repair. After the amputation, the nickname Chevy began to spread. My dad said the reason he changed his story was because if word got out that he'd lost his leg while working on someone's car, it would have hurt his auto repair business.

I often wondered who would take their car to a junkyard for repair? I realized there were things I was not going to understand at my age, but taking your car to a junkyard for service was kind of like going to a morgue for a physical, don't you think?

The one cool thing about the Caddy fort was its proximity to all of our houses. In the wintertime, when the days were much shorter, going all the way to the Dungeness fort meant most of your hang time was chewed up by the trip to and fro, so the Caddy fort made sense in a pinch. We could eat dinner, be at the Caddy for two games of Skat or maybe some Dino Board and still be home by the first flicker of the streetlights.

The Cadillac fort had one rule. No homework. Ever. You could not even talk about school or you would be fined. That was one rule I had no problem with. I hated homework because it always stressed me out, but Mom had a secret to help me deal with the stress of homework. The secret was to do your homework BEFORE it was due, not on the DAY it was due. Mom sure had a way of making sense of the world.

"I'm worried, you guys," Jaq said, climbing into the Caddy through the back window, which was her signature entrance into the fort.

"I told you we should've gone after him," Jimmy said. "Dude's probably got a fat lip from Tommy Osborne by now."

This was right about the time I rode up and power-slid to a stop just outside the fence.

"They gotta catch me first, Jimmy."

"What's up, Scooter?"

"How'd you get away?"

"Yeah man, what's the 9-1-1?" Jimmy added, which was answered with a series of double takes from the rest of us.

"What?" he replied. "Hello? It's the new phone number in case of emergency. Don't you pay attention to the news, Zippy?"

"Touché, Jimmy," Zippy replied. "Touché."

"What's going on, little brother?" Gary asked me as I scaled the fence and sat in the front seat, which had been turned around facing the backseat, so it was hard to call it the front seat, if you know what I mean.

Pulling the small metal cylinder from my belt, I placed it on the wooden milk crate coffee table before us.

"What the heck is that?" Jimmy asked, reaching out to pick it up.

Almost on cue, Zippy slapped Jimmy's hand like a mother guarding a freshly baked tray of chocolate chip cookies from her kids.

"What did you do that for?" Jimmy whined.

"Let me ask you somethin' there, Mr. Kool-Aid," Zippy said, challenging him. "What grade did you get in science class last year?"

"Oh, big whoop! You got an A. Doesn't make you an expert on really old ... metal ... thingies," Jimmy fired back. He was searching for a clever noun, but "old metal thingie" was all he could come up with.

"Well, it makes me smarter than you, so back off, Chumley. You might learn something."

For the next fifteen minutes, I told them about my discovery and my ultimate escape on the bike. I could see it in their faces! They were energized about the treasure again, especially Zippy who could not wait to open the cylinder lying on the milk crate before us.

"Wait, Zippy! Before you open it," Jimmy said, sitting up and holding his hands out like a referee, "we should take a moment. Right?"

"For what?" Zippy said, his hand about an inch away from picking up the cylinder.

"I don't know. It's just kinda cool if you think about it," Jimmy replied. "This thing might lead us to the treasure."

Jaq looked at me. I looked at Zippy, who quickly looked at Gary.

"Okay, we thought about it, now let's see what's inside," Gary said.

Jimmy did have a point, though. To imagine that we were the first to open the cylinder in over forty something years was indeed pretty cool. The thing was older than our parents, and we all knew they were ancient.

Zippy held the cylinder in one hand, and with the index finger and thumb of the other, he slowly twisted the cap. Dirt and corrosion from the small threads of the cap fell down like snowflakes. Carefully setting the cap down, he peered inside the mysterious metal cylinder.

"What is it?" I asked eagerly. "What do you see?"

Zippy held out his hand as he turned the cylinder upright. An old rolled up piece of parchment paper fell into his palm. The edges of the paper were weathered and frayed. It looked just like the map from *Treasure Island*.

"Saweet! … Unravel it."

"Whoa!"

"Cool!"

"Unravel it."

"I bet it's a map," Jimmy said, looking down at the map.

"Gee, thanks, Captain Obvious."

It never stopped between Jimmy and Zippy. Here we were in front of Jean Lafitte's lost treasure map, and those two still found time to bicker at each other.

Zippy acted like he was handling something from a museum, the way he carefully removed the cracked leather tie that kept the parchment rolled up. Slowly, using two Pixie Sticks from our candy stash under the backseat, he unrolled the parchment flat and we all peered down at it. As fate would have it, Jimmy and Zippy butted heads as they both leaned in for a closer look.

"Watch out!" Zippy said.

"Hey, you're not the boss of me. You ever think you might've been the one who bumped into me?"

"Well, I'm not the one with the big ol' bulbous head now, am I?" Zippy shot back. "Now back up, ya cow, you're hoggin' all the oxygen."

"Well, it's definitely some kind of map," Gary said, ignoring Jimmy and Zippy's constant bickering battle.

"Look at that!" Jaq said, pointing to a section of the small map where six figures stood on a hill, right above what looked like a river or stream.

"Don't touch it!" Zippy commanded, popping up from his crouched position over the map.

"All right. Geez! Don't blow a gasket," Jaq replied.

"Sorry, Jaq. It's just your hands … the acid from your skin … It might discolor the parchment."

"That would be bad," Jaq agreed.

"Yes. That would be bad."

Zippy smiled and continued to decipher the map. While Jaq wanted to be treated like one of the guys, we were all taught to be nice to girls, so unless provoked, she was left out of the back and forth jam of cut-downs.

"Is there an X-marks-the-spot?" Gary asked leaning in.

"I don't see one."

"That's because there isn't one," Zippy said in a defeated tone. "The map looks like it's incomplete."

Zippy was right. The map was incomplete. Every treasure map has an X-marks-the-spot, and from what we could tell, this one did not. Zippy raised his eyes from the map and looked directly at me.

"All right. Help me break this down, Scooter. You said Old Man Sheesley had the same infinity symbol around his neck as the one at the boat?"

"Yep. That's what gave me the idea to head back to the boat."

"Interesting," Zippy replied.

"Why is that interesting?" Gary asked.

"Because I'm guessing Old Man Sheesley has a map too. He found the first two keys. This here's from the third key, and so it seems logical that every key comes with a hidden map or something."

"All right! Cool! Let's go," Jaq said, sitting up.

"What do you mean, let's go? Go where?" Jimmy asked.

"Old Man Sheesley's house," Zippy answered. "Duh."

"Right. Okay," Jimmy said, laughing skeptically. "Let's just go knock on the door of the craziest man in town and get fed to his dog like all those runaway kids we keep hearing about. No, thank you. You can count me out, Buck Rogers. I ain't going."

"Fine, stay home. Who's in?" Zippy asked, looking around the table.

"In for what?"

"Operation Break-In," Zippy said with his all too familiar mischievous smile, which suddenly fell like a curtain at the end of a play. "Chevy's coming!" he yelled as he quickly grabbed the parchment before diving out the doors of the Caddy like some kind of superhero. I slowly turned and saw Hergenrader walking towards us with a metal baseball bat, poised and ready for destruction.

"Run!" I repeated the alert. One by one, we scrambled, falling all over each other to get out of the Caddy as fast as we could.

CRASH!

The metal bat came crashing down onto the roof of the Caddy, attacking our ears with its thundering velocity. Dropping the bat and reaching through the side windows of the Caddy, Hergenrader grabbed my baseball stirrups just as I was about to make a clean get-away.

"Grab my hand!" Gary shouted, reaching back for me.

Kicking and screaming, I latched onto Gary's hand and suddenly became the rope in a deadly game of tug-of-war. Gary was losing his battle against the older, stronger man, who had anger fueling his rickety frame. Jimmy returned and grabbed hold of my other hand.

"I got you now, you little squirt!"

"Pull!" Gary ordered.

"I am!" Jimmy replied, but they were quickly losing the battle for my life. I was being pulled through the side windows, into the clutches of the wicked one-legged monster of a man, Helmet "Chevy" Hergenrader. Just when it seemed like I was a goner for sure, I heard Jaq's voice rise up behind Hergenrader.

"Hey Chevy!" she yelled. "Over here, ya old man. Here Chevy, Chevy, Chevy."

Hergenrader froze. He stopped pulling my leg out of its socket to see Jaq standing ten feet behind him inside the junkyard. This gave Gary and Jimmy just enough leverage to pull me free of his greasy hands.

"Jaq, what are you doing?" I screamed as the guys pulled me out the other side of the Caddy.

"Come on, Chevy. You're not so tough!" she said, taunting him.

"Jaq! Get outta there!" Zippy yelled from the safety of the other side of the fence.

Hergenrader turned to face her. His wooden leg dug into the dirt below him like a bull preparing to rush a matador. Before I could utter a warning to Jaq, Hergenrader bolted forward faster than any of us ever thought he could move.

Thump! Stride ... Thump! Stride ...

"Run, Jaq! Run!" we all yelled, but Jaq stood still, waiting for Hergenrader to draw closer.

"What the heck is she doing?" Gary yelled.

Before anyone could answer, she dodged past Hergenrader like a wide receiver dodging a defensive back. When he tried to follow her expert lateral move, his wooden leg stuck in the dirt like a lawn dart, and he tumbled to the ground without it.

There was a momentary feeling of pity for the man, but this lasted only a few seconds because he crawled after her like a Green Beret on a mission. He grabbed his leg and put himself back together as Jaq quickly jumped over him and scaled the fence to a chorus of cheers from the rest of us. It was a masterful performance, and we slapped hands with her as though we had just won a baseball game.

Jumping on our bikes, we rode into town and gathered around the fountain in Town Square. Operation Break-In was on. The plan was we would go over to Old Man Sheesley's house and break in after nightfall. It would be the perfect time because every night, according to Jimmy, who lived down the street from him, Old Man Sheesley walked his dog at 9:45 p.m. like clockwork. He walked down Franklin Street to Water Street and stopped at Aldrich's Pub & Grocery for a single beer. My dad, who had stopped at Aldrich's Pub & Grocery more than a few times in his life, said Old Man Sheesley would sit at a small table near the front window to watch over his dog, which was tied to the parking meter outside. While drinking his one beer, he would scribble in an old leather notebook.

Knowing what I knew now, I could not help but wonder what was inside that old notebook of his. He never stayed for a second beer because Aldrich's Pub & Grocery closed every night at ten. After drinking his beer, he would walk back home. Zippy estimated the entire trip would take him around twenty-five minutes—which was more than enough time to break in, search his place and get out before he knew we were ever there.

With the plan set, we all hurried home to act as normal as we could. For some of us, that would be a tall order with our latest discovery buzzing around in our heads like a swarm of yellow jackets. For everything to work, we had to act like secret agents and not let on about what was happening in our lives. It had been a long and adventure-filled day, but the journey was not over. In fact, it was just beginning.

17

SHATTERED GLASS

Night was in bloom as the full moon began to dance across the waters of the bay. I awoke to the sensation of a spider crawling across my sleeping face. My eyes quickly snapped open and I sat up, hitting my head on the top bunk. Gary was hanging over the edge of our bunk beds, dragging a small piece of thread across my face. This was his idea of fun and games? Making me think a spider was going to crawl up my nose?

"What the heck are you doing?" I asked, but he jumped to the floor and clasped his hand over my mouth.

"Shhhhh! You'll wake Mom and Dad," he said in a hushed whisper. "Time to go."

"Go? What? Where?" I mumbled, disoriented from the sudden leap into consciousness.

"Come on. Get dressed. We gotta get movin'," he said, grabbing a flashlight from the desk, which sat next to our custom-made bunk beds.

During the off-season of salmon fishing, Dad liked to keep himself busy by building things around the house. He had made our pool table in the den from a mail-order kit he found in the back of the Sears catalog, and just a few months ago, he had made our bunk beds from his own design.

Shaped like the letter L, one bed sat on top of two large drawers, and the head of the lower bed fit into a small cave under the foot of the top bed. This little cave was where I slept, and it was pretty cool at night. I had plastered the ceiling of my little cave with glow-in-the-dark stars, and before going to bed each night, I would look up and dream about my future. I would visualize myself playing for the New York Mets. Have you ever felt that way when you're looking up at the stars? Like you could do anything you wanted with your life? Dad always used to say if you can see it, you can achieve it. I liked that because I could definitely see myself playing for the Mets one day.

Climbing from our bedroom window, we quietly made our way to the garage, hopped onto our bikes and rode off under the cover of night.

Arriving in the trees that surrounded Old Man Sheesley's property, we met Zippy and Jaq, who were already there doing surveillance.

"Where's Jimmy?" I asked, slowing to a stop next to them.

"Late as usual," Jaq replied.

Scanning the exterior of the old house with binoculars, which was overkill because the house was only fifty yards across the massive green lawn, Zippy suddenly sat up from his crouched position next to a tree.

"There he is!" he announced in a loud whisper. "Hide!"

"Who? Jimmy?" I asked, looking around.

"Old Man Sheesley!" Zippy said, ripping me from my bike down to the ground as Jaq and Gary ducked for cover behind another tree. As I landed on the ground, I peered through the bushes to see Old Man Sheesley looking right in our direction. Koya, his giant Saint Bernard, began to bark just as a watchdog should. I wondered if our mission was compromised before it even had a chance to begin.

We held absolutely still for a good minute, afraid even to look up. When I finally did, I saw Jimmy crest Franklin Street in silhouette. He was about to turn onto the trail, which would lead him to our location. If Old Man Sheesley saw him, our mission would be thwarted.

"Oh no," I said.

"What?" Zippy whispered back to me.

"Here comes Jimmy," Gary said, following my gaze.

"He's going to blow it."

"Come on, Jimmy. Look up. Look up and see Old Man Sheesley," Gary said coaching him, but Jimmy, as usual, was oblivious to his surroundings.

At the last split second, luck arrived in our favor when Old Man Sheesley gave up on his paranoid instincts and crossed to his beat-up '49 Ford pickup. When he opened the door, Koya leapt into the front seat with a single hop. Seconds later, Jimmy arrived at our location, clueless of the jeopardy he had nearly thrust us into. Old Man Sheesley climbed into the driver's seat and shut the door.

"Why are you guys hiding?" he asked.

"Get down, dummy!" Gary said as he reached up and pulled Jimmy to the ground. "Look," he said, pointing Jimmy's face towards to the taillights of the pickup as the engine fired to life with a popping backfire.

"I thought you said he walks to the bar every night?" Zippy asked.

"He does."

"Well, does that look like walking to you, numbskull?"

"You almost blew the entire mission. What took you so long?"

"Don't have a cow, man. My dad took forever to fall asleep, and he's still in his chair, so I don't know how long I can stay. Were you even going to wait for me?"

"Show up on time, or be left behind. That's the rule," I reminded him as the pickup backfired a second time before rolling out of the driveway onto Franklin Street.

The headlights raked across our position and it was like a game of Duck, Duck, Goose the way our heads shot down into the bushes at the last split second.

When Old Man Sheesley's truck was finally out of sight, Gary climbed to his feet and announced it was time to go. Now, I was not sure if it was the shadows of the night or my own imagination, but the closer I got to the old Lafitte mansion, the more haunted it looked.

"Jimmy, you stay here and stand guard." Gary turned and pointed.

"Why do I have to stand guard?"

"Last to show, last to go," we all said in unison.

"If you see someone coming, give us a head's up," Zippy said, moving across the grass.

"What kind of head's up?" Jimmy whispered after us.

"Jeez, man, figure one out," Zippy said as we began to slink our way across the massive lawn.

At this point, my mind wandered to last summer when

our parents had taken us to Disneyland. I had a great time, don't get me wrong, but that Haunted Mansion scared the living daylights out of me. I was only twelve back then, but I had nightmares for a good week after. Gary called me a scaredy-cat, but again, I was twelve years old, and I got over it. Breaking into Old Man Sheesley's house was different. At least when I was at Disneyland, I knew I was not going to die from being scared. Tonight I had no idea what I was about to walk into. I had no idea if the runaway child rumor was true or not. I hoped with all my heart it was not.

"Zippy? What's our new time window?" Gary whispered back to him.

"With him driving? I'm gonna guess we got ten minutes."

With the mission shortened and the stakes suddenly raised, we were lucky to find one of the front windows unlatched. Like a game of follow the leader, we crawled into the darkness of the house.

Looking back to give Jimmy the thumbs up, I saw him reacting to his own runaway imagination. His head shot to the left, then to the right. I did not blame him, because being out there, all alone in the dark, was not somewhere I'd want to be either. Safety in numbers was my motto.

The beams of our flashlights cut through the soupy darkness like a hot knife into a cold stick of butter. The shadows of the room were heavy, drifting off into a pitch-black abyss at every corner. Stacks of books were littered about the cluttered space. With the ornate wood paneling covering the walls, which were carved to perfection, it felt like we were inside an old pirate ship. I thought that was pretty cool, but just as I was becoming comfortable with my surroundings, a voice suddenly shattered our cat burglar-like silence.

"I'm going to whistle," Jimmy said as his head poked through the open window.

"Great. Good for you. Now go stand guard," Gary said, pushing his face out the window.

"Oh my god! What was that?" Jimmy asked, popping his head in through the open window. We all froze, but heard nothing.

"It's just your imagination. Now go stand guard; you're wasting time"

"No, wait!" Jaq said, speaking up. "He's right, I heard something too."

We strained to listen for some kind of sound—any kind of sound—but again, we heard nothing except the chattering of the crickets off in the distance.

"All right, let's not get crazy and start imagining things that aren't there," Gary said. "Jimmy, keep your eyes peeled. The rest of you, get to work. We don't have much time."

"We should've left him behind when we had the chance," Zippy said, scanning the bookshelves in front of him as his words trailed off into silence.

"You find something?" I asked, recognizing the slowing cadence of his sentence. We gathered around his flashlight to see newspaper clippings and pictures of Ms. Benson, the old librarian.

"Looks like someone's got a crush on the librarian," Zippy said with a smile.

"More like a stalker crush," Jaq said, setting the pictures on the table.

"What are you talking about?"

"Scooter, look at these pictures. She obviously didn't know he was taking her picture."

"So?"

"So, it's creepy. Someone watching her, taking pictures of her, and she doesn't even know it? I'm telling you, that's super creepy."

"Well, maybe he's shy?" I said in Old Man Sheesley's defense, which caught me off-guard for a second. Why was I defending him? Then it occurred to me that Ms. Benson was important to him the way Brandy Larson was important to me.

"Consider the source, Jaq," Gary said, moving away from the huddle. "Guy's a freakazoid. I mean, look at this dump."

"Looks like he's not only taking pictures. Look at this," Zippy said, peering through the telescope pointing out the front window.

"Where's it pointed? I asked.

"The baseball field."

"He's watching games from here?"

"And look at this," Gary said, thumbing through an open notebook lying on a side table. "He's keeping stats on us and everything." Slowly, Gary began to read from the pages: "Scott needs to stop swinging at high pitches and trust in his swing."

"It doesn't say that."

"Right here in black and white, brother." Gary placed his finger on the page to show me it was indeed written in black and white.

Looking to get the attention off of my strikeout record, I began to read the next entry without even thinking about what it said: "John White is doing great, considering he lost his father. I worry about the kid. I hope he's okay."

"What?" Zippy said, shining his flashlight on the page.

"This guy's right out of an episode of 'Creature Features,'" Jaq said, growing leery. "I don't think I wanna be here anymore."

"What's that?" I said, directing our attention to a sliver of light coming from behind a bookcase. Moving closer, we scanned the large, built-in bookcase.

"Shut your flashlights off!" Zippy ordered.

One by one, our flashlights winked off. Moving in closer, we discovered there was a light source coming from behind the bookcase itself. Before we could register the discovery before us, a rustling sound erupted from the hallway.

"Did you hear that?" Zippy said.

The rustling sound was undeniable, because everybody had heard it this time.

"See, I told you!" Jaq said in a loud whisper. "What the heck is it?"

Quickly rising from our huddle in front of the bookcase, Gary and Zippy entered the hallway to investigate. Not to be left behind, Jaq latched onto my arm and we slowly followed behind them. With each step, the old wooden floor creaked from our combined weight, and the shadows of the room seemed to dance in our imagination. I was not sure if it was the fear of this unknown sound rushing through me, but I could feel my senses begin to heighten. The dusty smell of the living room intensified, and I could feel my heart beating into my fingertips.

My eyes focused into the long hallway, where a light from under a mysterious door bled into the soupy darkness before us. Gary and Zippy were nodding back and forth to each other to see who wanted to go first. Of course, each thought the other should proceed, but when a shadow passed in front of the light, everyone stiffened with fear.

"Someone's here!" Zippy whispered in a panic-filled rush of adrenalin.

As we turned to make a run for it, a rock suddenly shattered the living room window into a million pieces.

Shards of broken glass fell to the hardwood floor like a tipped-over box of Rice Krispies.

Jimmy's face popped into the open window frame, filled with undeniable terror.

"He's home!"

The rumble of the old pickup grew louder as it pulled into the driveway.

"Hide!"

"Hide? Run!" Gary ordered as he raced out of the hallway and dove through the open window, followed quickly by Jaq and Zippy. I went back for Old Man Sheesley's notebook about our baseball games. I wanted to find out what he'd written about us, but when I dashed around the edge of the couch, I ran right into a side table and went down hard. The leather notebook slid from my hands and pages flew into the air like confetti. Looking up, I saw the doorknob of the back door begin to turn. I was trapped.

18

DRIPPING WITH BLOOD

With my heart pounding like a jackhammer, I ducked into the pantry of Old Man Sheesley's kitchen. It was dark, and it smelled of soda crackers that were probably older than I was. I was breathing so loudly that I thought the sound might betray my location, so I tried to calm myself, but that was easier said than done.

Peering through the crack of the pantry door, I watched as the old metal hinges of the back door echoed throughout the house like a horror film. Koya entered first, pushing past the aging legs of Old Man Sheesley as he entered. The massive paws of the beast, which could easily be mistaken for the paws of a black bear in the dark, thundered against the hardwood floor with excitement. His nose was wet and his mouth was covered with slobber, an unfortunate characteristic of Saint Bernards.

I held my breath, trying to calm my beating heart as Old Man Sheesley walked right in front of the pantry door. His long, ratty coat danced behind him like the cape of a dark knight. Hunched over and breathing heavily, he swung two large burlap sacks onto the butcher-block countertop.

What's inside those bags and what's that dark liquid dripping from them? I thought.

When I leaned closer into the crack of the door, my heart just about stopped as I realized that the dark liquid dripping from the sacks was—blood?

I have to get out of here, I screamed to myself, but I was not going anywhere. I was trapped.

Moving to the large dining table that looked like a piece of furniture from medieval times, Old Man Sheesley removed his coat and swung it over a wooden chair. He suddenly froze, and this was a bad thing. What was he looking at?

My question was quickly answered as he walked over to the broken glass of the window, compliments of Jimmy's errant throw. In an instant, Old Man Sheesley's boot slammed to the hardwood floor, crushing the broken pieces into a fine powder of glass. He was angry, which did not help my predicament.

My eyes shot to the back door, and I saw that it was still slightly ajar. Maybe I could make a run for it while he was preoccupied. But as I considered the thought, Old Man Sheesley entered my line of sight and kicked the back door shut, dashing any hopes of my escape.

The old man grunted and moved to a kitchen drawer as Koya circled around him with anticipation. Chunks of slobber dripped to the floor as he looked up at his master. If I had not known better, I would have said the dog was smiling, but I could not take my eyes off those burlap bags, which were now oozing blood down the sides of the countertop.

Pulling on plastic gloves, Old Man Sheesley looked like a surgeon about to operate—but on what? What was in those bloody bags? My thoughts were screaming at me now, demanding answers, but I had none. I was so scared I did not know what to think. How was I going to get out of there?

Old Man Sheesley grabbed the bags and emptied them onto the counter. Bloody chunks of meat and bone fell with a horrifying *SLAP!* onto the butcher-block counter. He grabbed a meat-clever from a drawer. Arching it high into the air, Old Man Sheesley cut completely through the bloody flesh with a single blow.

A pulse of fear shot through my body and I gasped for air without even knowing it. Koya's dripping mouth snapped shut like a mousetrap, and his massive head jerked in my direction. With blood dripping from his deadly clever, Old Man Sheesley looked down at his dog, which was now like a hunting dog focused on an innocent pheasant hiding in the high grass.

As the old man walked out of view, the sound of his footsteps receded into the hallway. Was he leaving? I did not wait for an answer. I knew this was my only chance for escape, but Koya's steely gaze was imprisoning me in my hiding place. His mouth slowly opened, showing his jagged teeth, stained with the blood of who-knows-what. Then the large beast began to growl. I was not sure if I was even breathing at that point, because I was more scared than I had ever been in my entire life. Disneyland was nothing compared to this. This was as real as it got.

Thinking fast, I knew a dog's bite would not be as horrible as my arm being chopped off, courtesy of the meat clever, so I bolted for the door. One step. Two steps. There was the door. I was close, but not close enough. Upon seeing me, Koya's massive claws dug for traction into the hardwood floor. He was like a teenager peeling out as a traffic light turned green. Splinters of the wooden floor flew into the air behind him, but he had not gained an inch on me. Not yet, which is why I knew I was going to make it. Three steps. Four steps. I was almost to the door. Five steps. Six.

I reached out for the door knob, grabbed it, and turned as fast as I could, which was right about the time Koya's wheels caught up to his massive strides. He shot forward like a rocket ship. I swung open the door, and just as I took a step into freedom, I was lifted into the air and slammed to the ground. I saw more stars than I'd see during a night camping in the Olympic Forest. My eyes grew heavy, trying to focus, but everything faded and went dark. I felt like I was dying.

Moments later, I awoke to the sounds of Koya's jaws, chomping through chunks of flesh. I was cold, and I could not feel my legs. It had happened.

Koya is now eating my legs, I thought as I gradually regained consciousness.

But—what was that soft feeling behind my head? I reached back and felt—a pillow! A pillow?

My eyes focused and saw Old Man Sheesley stirring a cup of tea at the counter. His back was to me, but I felt his eyes on me, somehow. He tapped the spoon on the edge of the cup more than a few times, as if he wanted to gain my attention. He'd captured it. He placed the spoon on a perfectly folded paper napkin. His movements were slow and deliberate, which only added to the creep factor. After a long exhale, he turned and sat down at the kitchen table.

What is that sticking off the edge of the table? I asked myself. *Is that a—double-barreled shotgun?*

My eyes widened even further and my heart started to race again. I had to get out of here, but I could not move. I was frozen right there, lying on the floor, which felt cold against my back.

The old man slurped his tea, which trickled down his long, gray beard like a waterfall. His dark eyes finally lifted and focused on me.

"Did you break my window?" he growled.

"What?" I said, sitting up with my head still spinning.

"I said, did you break my window?" he asked again, repositioning the shotgun to make sure I saw it.

How could I miss it? It was double-barreled.

"No. Well. *I* didn't," I replied, looking up at the pile of bloody meat on the counter, and then down to Koya, whose mouth was dripping with blood as if he'd been chewing on thumb tacks or something.

"Hold onto your imagination, young man."

"I'm sorry?" I replied, snapping out of it.

"I know the rumors you kids spread. If you'd care to investigate past hearsay, you'd know he's eating scraps from the butcher shop, and nothing more," he said, providing clarification.

At this point, Koya looked at me with his bloody teeth, as if to remind me that while his attention was on the bowl of bloody meat before him, he could pounce on me in a moment's notice. I would not have dreamed of questioning his power or authority.

"He's a really big Saint Bernard," I said nervously as I watched the dog chomp down on a large piece of bloody meat.

"*She's* a Bernese Mountain Dog."

"Sure looks like a Saint Bernard."

"Well, she isn't. Saint Bernards are brown and white. Does she look brown and white to you?" he said, growing impatient. "Now, what do you want?"

Even though he was not the friendliest guy in town, I was surprised by how eloquently Old Man Sheesley spoke. But then it occurred to me that I had never heard him speak before. The rumors about him made me assume he would talk in grumbling sentence fragments like some kind of monster. He did not. As far as I could tell, he was not a monster at all. A monster would not have propped my head up with a pillow.

"Why do you have pictures of Ms. Benson in your house?"

"And this is why you choose to break my window? To ask me such a question?" he asked, setting his cup of tea on the table to make a point.

"What? No. *That* was an accident. We—"

"We?" he snapped in return, his voice booming again as he looked around the room for the others. "Where are they?"

"Long gone, I guess. They're afraid of you," I replied, slowly climbing to my feet with an eye still on Koya's bloody jaws.

"And you?"

"You're not so bad, I guess," I said, taking a step closer.

"You don't know me."

"My mom says we shouldn't judge someone if we don't know them," I replied with an eye on the shotgun, wondering if I should heed the advice of my mother or judge what I was seeing and make a run for it. Anyone who keeps a shotgun on the kitchen table was someone I did not want any part of.

"Your mother taught you this?"

"Yes sir. Dad, too. I think they're different than most parents. At least that's what our friends say."

I slowly took a seat across from him at the large table. Now my movements were slow and deliberate, because I did not want to alarm the old man, or Koya for that matter.

It was strange sitting here with him, because he was different from what I had expected. Though his face was wrinkled and old, there was an innocence about him, which made me feel bad for the thoughts I had about him before this moment.

"They sort of let us do what we want," I continued.

"Does that include breaking my window?" he asked, leaning forward again, but I did not answer the question.

I merely looked around the room at all the books I had not seen when the place was shrouded in darkness.

"I guess you like to read, huh?" I asked, picking up a book from a stack on the table.

He rose quickly, grabbed the book and placed it back in the stack as if he was adhering to some sort of complex filing system.

"Robert Lewis Stevenson is my favorite," I said. "Ms. Benson helps me with the big words." I paused for a second, continuing to look around. "Is she the reason you have all these books?"

His dark, sullen eyes just looked at me, which made me even more nervous as a long, uncomfortable moment of silence passed.

I finally looked away and took in my surroundings again. The place was cluttered, but somehow organized. Everything had its perfect place, including Polaroid pictures of Ms. Benson on the steps of the library, announcing the discovery of the third key.

"So, you like Ms. Benson?"

He did not answer.

"You ever get afraid she might not like you back?" I asked. "Does that ever happen to older people?"

"Why don't you tell me why you broke my window?" he asked, finishing the last sip of his tea.

"My mom says that when I change the subject, it usually means I'm hiding from the truth."

"Well, you have a smart mother. Good for you! Now what do you want?" he demanded.

"The thing around your neck ... the pendant?"

"What about it?" he replied, rising to put his cup in the kitchen sink, which was overflowing with dirty dishes.

I guess he did not like doing dishes, either.

"We found a piece of the map," I said directly, hoping to coax some information out of him, but he did not say a word.

Old Man Sheesley just turned around and looked straight at me. If I had not known any better, I would have said a smile began to cross his aging face. It was at this moment that I knew Zippy was right, and we were close to discovering the lost treasure of Jean Lafitte.

TREASURE TIP

Telling the truth is easier than telling a lie.

19

A DIFFERENT MAN

Hidden in the bushes, under the rocks and beneath the fallen trees of the forest that lined Old Man Sheesley's property, the crickets of summer had begun their nightly chorus. The air was still and warm.

It was approaching 10:30 p.m., and even though Jimmy claimed that his dad might wake up any second, he stood before me, digging his heels into our debate of should-we-stay-or-should-we-go? So far, I was outnumbered four to one. I agreed that a covert spy mission was more fun than actually talking to the man you wanted to spy on, but

I stood my ground. I told them Old Man Sheesley knew something, and I was going back in, with or without them.

It took about ten minutes to convince everyone to come inside and listen to Old Man Sheesley talk about the lost treasure of Jean Lafitte—everyone, except Jimmy, of course, who said he was going home. I knew he was afraid, and that was okay; in fact, it was more than okay. The more I thought about it, the more I knew Sheriff Finn would knock on our door first to see if Jimmy was with us. Opening our bedroom door, Dad would only find the pillows we'd stuffed under the covers to make it look like we were still in bed. I was certain we would be grounded for the rest of our lives, so maybe it was a good idea for Jimmy to go home.

As we approached the mansion, we were surprised to see the back door propped open, welcoming us. Holding the doorjamb, I leaned forward and scanned the interior. There was no sign of Old Man Sheesley, his shotgun or Koya, for that matter. The place was still as could be. That made me nervous.

Gary, Zippy and Jaq were huddled behind me on the stoop like a team of mountain climbers, tethered together with a short safety rope.

"Where's he at?" Gary asked in a hushed tone as he reached out and pushed my shoulder, challenging me for answers.

"Stop pushing me. I'm not the man's babysitter," I replied, stepping inside with momentary confidence. "Hello?" I called out, pausing for a second when it occurred to me that I did not know Old Man Sheesley's first name. I turned to the others. "What's his first name?"

"Old Man Sheesley," Zippy said with a laugh.

"I can't call him that."

I took another cautious step inside the spooky house. "Sir? Mister Sheesley?" My voice echoed, but again, there was no answer. My mind started to race because this was odd. Where had he gone? Before I could answer my own question, a short, muffled scream shot up behind me. Spinning around, I saw that Jaq was staring at the bloody meat cleaver on the counter. I tried to gently explain the dripping meat cleaver, but she looked past me and screamed again. I spun around and saw Old Man Sheesley standing in the darkened hallway. He stepped closer, still cloaked in the shadows like some kind of spooky monster.

I could feel everyone take a step backward, reconsidering their decision to come inside, especially Jaq, who was breathing so hard it sounded like a scuba diver was right behind me. I slowly turned my gaze towards Old Man Sheesley, who had yet to speak. This guy seriously needed to work on his people skills, because he was anything but a welcoming host. Then, it occurred to me that we were probably the first houseguests he had ever had in the old Lafitte mansion.

"We're all here," I said, my voice shaking a little. Stepping closer, the old man looked us over like a drill sergeant examining a set of new recruits. I scanned the room for Koya, but he was nowhere to be found. Then, from behind a closed door in the kitchen, we heard a loud bark.

"Are you coming in?" Old Man Sheesley asked, looking back into the room.

"Are you asking us, or the dog?" I replied.

"I'm asking Jimmy."

He snapped his head towards the broken window, and Jimmy ducked out of sight. It was as if Koya had sensed Jimmy's presence somehow and alerted the old man. That was really creepy.

"How did he see him?" Jaq whispered to Gary.

"Jimmy. He … um … he has to get home," I replied, trying to act normal, which, given the circumstances, was nearly impossible. "His dad's asleep in front of the television."

"Brainwashed like the rest of the town," Old Man Sheesley muttered as he opened a cupboard to retrieve a tattered leather notebook from a shelf. I wondered if this was the same notebook that my dad had mentioned. If it was, I could not help but think it might be his diary or something. Maybe it was a research book about the treasure. I did not know, but my curiosity was bubbling up again.

Holding the book in his hands like a preacher preparing to give a sermon, Old Man Sheesley flipped through a couple of pages, looked us over and flipped to another page before reading something quietly to himself. Then he shut the book tightly and addressed us.

"Perhaps you should go outside and convince Jimmy I mean him no harm," he said to me, in what seemed like a more pleasant tone than before.

"I already tried."

"Then try harder," he said, looking directly at me and speaking in yet another tone of voice. His quick mood change threw us off balance and rekindled our previous fear of the old man. I was glad Jimmy was not there anymore. At least someone could explain our last known whereabouts if we went missing.

"Jimmy's just a scaredy-cat, that's all," Zippy said, breaking the silence.

"If he could field the ball like a cat, maybe you could win more games," the old man replied through an empty gaze.

After another long beat of uncomfortable silence, Old Man Sheesley finally spoke again. "Very well. This way," he grumbled as he turned to walk towards the living room.

His step was heavy, lumbering—almost lethargic. The wooden floor creaked under his weight. I could not help but notice that something was missing from this man. The obvious answer would be a wife or a family, but it was deeper than that. It felt like he was missing something inside.

As we followed him, Gary nudged me to get my attention.

"What the heck is going on?" he whispered.

"Yeah. Guy gives me the heebie-jeebies," Jaq added quietly.

"Oh, and Scott," Old Man Sheesley said without turning around, "you should listen to your brother."

"I'm sorry?"

"For what?" he said, turning around and setting off a chain reaction as if we were a line of dominos. Jaq bumped into Zippy, Zippy into Gary and Gary into me, jolting me forward a step.

"What?"

"You keep saying you're sorry. Why are you apologizing?"

"Well, I ..."

"Other than breaking the window, you've done nothing wrong, right?" he asked from the shadows of the living room.

"I ... just ... didn't hear you," I said, stumbling on my words, slightly confused by his mysterious presence and sudden questions. This guy was indeed odd.

"Then say, 'I didn't hear you.' Don't apologize. Be mindful of the words you choose in communication. Each word has meaning, and words like 'I can't,' 'I'm afraid,' 'This is overwhelming' or, in your case, 'I'm sorry' indicate uncertainty and weakness."

"Okay, I didn't hear you," I replied, almost challenging him, but he talked right over me.

"However, if you did care to apologize, you could start with apologizing to your teammates, which is why I said you should listen to your brother."

I froze and did not know what to say, so I came up with something clever. "What?" I'm sure my English teacher would have been proud, because of all the words I could have used for an inquiry, I chose the elaborate and ever expansive "what."

"Gary gives you advice—tells you to lay off those high fastballs—but you continue to swing for the fences," the old man said. "Scott, the home run is the most overrated and difficult thing to accomplish in baseball. It cannot be forced."

He paused for effect, making sure his words sank in. It was a bit unnerving the way he used our first names as if we had been friends for years. We had not. In fact, we were anything but friends with the scraggly, gray-bearded stranger standing before us.

"We all want to be great," he continued. "That's the one thing that connects us all: our drive for excellence. Even Jimmy out there, hiding in the bushes somewhere, wants to be great, but negative thoughts wedge their way in and destroy our dreams. Somewhere, deep inside, you don't believe you can hit a home run if you just swing normally, so you force it and swing for the fences. But what happens? You fail. You fail because when you force something, you become tense, and when you're tense, you miss out on the very thing you've set out to accomplish."

Suddenly, the man became quiet, as if wondering why he had just leapt into a lecture about greatness with a group of kids who had broken his window. He was hard to figure out. He was scary one minute and helpful the next. I knew everybody was different, but this guy was weird. Weird and unpredictable.

"Enough about hitting home runs," he growled. "Follow me, and I'll show you what you've come here to see."

TREASURE TIP

The harder you try, the harder it gets.

20

THE SECRET ROOM

It had been the longest day of my life. Thinking about this morning, our discovery at the Dungeness River, the battle with Tommy for the third key to the treasure, the water balloon attack and, of course, losing our playoff game was like trying to remember what I did last summer on any given day.

My eyes were growing heavy, and I was not sure what I had gotten us into, but there we were, inside the house of the strangest man in all of Port Townsend, about to see something he claimed we were looking for.

Arriving at the same curious bookcase we had discovered earlier, Old Man Sheesley paused, looked back at us and reached high up onto the top shelf. At that moment, the same mysterious rustling sound from the hallway jolted us back more than a step. Seeing the panic on our faces, Old Man Sheesley looked down the hallway and back at us.

"It's okay. Nothing to fear!"

"Who's behind that door?" Gary demanded.

"I assure you, it's nothing like what you imagine."

"Then why don't you open the door and let us see?" Zippy asked.

"Because I'm not the one who wants it opened."

Gary pushed Zippy's shoulder from behind.

"What are you pushing me for?"

"Open it."

"You open it."

"It was your idea."

"Oh, like you don't want to see what's behind the door?"

"Why don't you open it together?" Old Man Sheesley said, putting a stop to the debate.

Exchanging looks back and forth, neither Zippy nor Gary made a move towards the door because we all knew the rumors about the runaways. As the debate raged on, none of us noticed that Jaq had moved and was standing before the door. Grabbing the doorknob, she looked back to me as if to say goodbye in case something terrible happened. The girl was fearless.

Just as she turned the knob, the same shadow we had seen earlier passed in front of the light. Jaq screamed and bolted to the safety of our little crowd. Turning our attention back to the hallway, we saw something move behind the door until finally, a burst of energy shot through. Three Bernese Mountain Dog puppies bounded our way.

"As I said before," Old Man Sheesley continued, standing over us, "imagining fearful things and jumping to conclusions will always get the best of you."

As Gary and Zippy tried to make sense out of Old Man Sheesley's advice, Jaq and I wasted no time before we scooped the puppies up in our arms. While one puppy licked my face, I watched Old Man Sheesley turn his attention back to the bookcase.

Reaching up to a high shelf, his hand brushed across several books before coming to rest on a copy of *Treasure Island*. He tipped the book as if it was on a hinge, and we all heard something click. The old man smiled. Then, using his foot, he tipped out a copy of *Huckleberry Finn* located on the bottom shelf. The combination of the two books tipping out caused the bookcase to pop open like the doors of a magnetic stereo cabinet.

The door creaked from the weight of the books, and dust particles shot into the light like a swarm of fruit flies. It was an eerie sight, this hidden door. It was so eerie that my mind began to race with troubling thoughts. Where was that shotgun of his? Why would anyone keep a secret room in their house? What did he use it for? Would there be some horrific discovery of a runaway kid hanging from the ceiling in a dark corner, dead as a doornail?

Peering inside like a group of kids at a zoo, we saw a small desk crowded in the corner of a tight space. There was no dead body. There were no bags of body parts. In fact, there was nothing sinister about the room at all. The only sinister thing about all of this was the runaway thoughts we had about Old Man Sheesley.

But then, I'm certain the boundless and carefree energy of a puppy could diffuse just about anything, especially fear. I was not alone, because Jaq was so busy talking to the puppy cradled in her hands about how cute he was and how smelly his puppy breath was that she too had forgotten the purpose of our visit. Puppies have a way of doing that, I guess.

"Hey! You two!" Gary said, reminding us of why we were here. "Enough with the puppies."

However much we loved the puppies and their unconditional love, Gary was right. We had to focus. Placing the puppies on the floor, Jaq and I watched them chase each other into the kitchen.

Turning our attention back to the small secret room, we saw that all four walls were covered with tattered maps, newspaper clippings about the *Keys of Lafitte* treasure hunt and failed solutions to the ciphers that had appeared in the newspaper over the years. One thing was certain: this guy was a serious treasure-hunting enthusiast. The gun rack on the far wall did throw a veil of concern over the excitement of discovery, but he did live in a forest, and this was the Pacific Northwest. It was not uncommon for a stray black bear to wander out of the hills for food, so I imagine the shotguns were for his protection.

"So ... tell me. How did you solve the third cipher?" Old Man Sheesley asked, turning to Zippy and blocking our view of the mysterious room.

When Zippy remained silent, Gary leaned forward and nudged him as if to say it was okay to answer the question.

"I ... used the Vigenère Cipher and the Rail Fence Cipher," Zippy replied as if his attention was elsewhere, because it was.

He was fascinated by what he saw plastered on the walls of the hidden room. We all were. Zippy tilted his head to the side to look past Old Man Sheesley, who simply nodded and said, "Of course. Good thinking, John."

"It's Zippy," he said. "My name is Zippy."

Old Man Sheesley moved into the small room, which was crowded with more research books. It was like a mini library, the way the books were stacked against the walls.

"This is really cool," Gary said, looking up to Old Man Sheesley, but the old man was preoccupied. His mind had drifted elsewhere, but just as fast as it had drifted away, it returned, and he looked directly at me.

"Now, let's get a look at that map of yours," he said, extending his long, rickety arm.

From the quick looks I received from the others, it occurred to me that I had mistakenly forgotten to tell them I had confessed we were in possession of the third map.

"Is there a problem?" he asked, sensing the confusion and mistrust displayed by the others.

"No," Zippy replied, looking at me as he pulled the cylinder from his pocket.

If looks could kill, I would have been a dead man walking. Reaching out, I took the cylinder, but not before Zippy jabbed against me to make sure I noticed that he was not happy. I noticed, but I took the cylinder from him with a jab of my own before placing it in Old Man Sheesley's wrinkled hand.

As he moved away from us, the old man scanned the cylinder, fascinated. Slowly, he emptied the parchment scroll into his hand. From the way he smiled at the scrap of parchment, it was obvious he was off in his own private world again. There appeared to be an uncomfortable obsession in the way he examined the furled paper, as if it held some sort of secret power over him.

Like a bolt of lightning, he snapped out of his daydream and realized we were all staring at him. He shook himself as if the moment that had just passed was nothing—but it was something. Something was very odd about this man besides the obvious things we already knew. His eyes hid behind his drooping eyelids as he carefully unrolled the delicate piece of parchment paper. He stared down at it as if he was hypnotized, taking in every detail the map conveyed. Moving to the wall behind him, he flipped on a small overhead work light.

Zippy's eyes grew wide, but I could not see what Old Man Sheesley was doing. Shifting my feet, I moved in for a closer look. It was unbelievable. Old Man Sheesley carefully fit our map into place with two other pieces of parchment tacked to the wall. The maps fit together like pieces of a jigsaw puzzle. Acting like it was nothing, Old Man Sheesley faced us again.

"This is it? This is all you found?"

"Well ... yeah."

"There wasn't a note ... accompanying the map?"

"No note, just the parchment you see there," Zippy answered. "Was there a note with the other two maps?"

Old Man Sheesley did not answer. He simply scanned the three maps on the wall then opened the top drawer of the small desk behind him. Pulling out a large magnifying glass, he studied the maps closely. It was obvious that the fourth and final parchment would complete a much larger treasure map.

I could not believe it. There we were, staring at an almost complete map of the lost treasure of Jean Lafitte.

"What do you see?" we asked eagerly.

"I see another dead end," he replied, filled with defeat. "Without the fourth piece, it's useless."

"Mind if I take a look?" Zippy asked, stepping forward.

Old Man Sheesley considered the request for a moment before handing over the magnifying glass. Zippy stepped up to the wall, pressed his face into the large lens and began to inspect the three sections of the map.

"What do you mean, dead end?" I asked.

But Old Man Sheesley did not answer. He just looked us over, thinking, deciding whether he should say anything more. After what seemed like an eternity had passed, he opened another drawer of his desk and retrieved an additional piece of parchment paper, sealed in a plastic bag. It looked just like the others, but this piece was much larger. It was about the same size as the notebook paper we used at school.

"Because of this," he said.

"What's that?" Jaq asked, stepping closer.

Old Man Sheesley began to read from the parchment encased in the plastic bag:

Congratulations!

You have started the greatest treasure hunt known to man. I wish I could tell you that you are in for riches beyond your imagination, but I will say this: you are not. The treasure you seek lies within. You are the grand explorer of your own life, the ultimate treasure of all. Learn. Grow. Expand your idea of who you are so you can become more of who you are meant to be.

I say this because you are a gift to mankind. Do not waste your life looking for something that is not to be found. The lost treasure of my great-grandfather, Jean Lafitte, is indeed lost. I began the Keys of Lafitte treasure hunt to teach those who follow it that life is the ultimate treasure. Cherish it. Love your families. Love your friends.

Curiosity will persist, and other keys to the "lost treasure" will be found, but it is up to you to give those who find these keys the gift of life.

It is up to you to shed light on the lost treasure.
You will share with them this letter, but secrecy
is the duty for all who discover the clues.
This hunt was enacted to bring families
and friends closer together—nothing more.
Truly yours, in the hunt to become more,

—Jacques Pierre Lafitte

"I knew it was a hoax," Jimmy said, arriving from the darkness of the living room behind us.

"Then you have missed the meaning of the letter, Jimmy," Old Man Sheesley said. "I'm sorry to have to tell you this, but riches come from hard work. Nothing in this life is free. There is no pot of gold at the end of the rainbow, despite your dreams of one."

"You got this house for free, didn't you?" Jaq inquired. "Sure sounds like a pot of gold to me."

"Yes, Jacqueline, but look around. I am alone. Having a big house does not bring happiness, my young friend. Achieving happiness is up to each of you—and it's not about what you can *get* from life. It's what you *bring* to it."

"What are these figures here?" Zippy asked with his face pressed to the large magnifying glass, practically ignoring our conversation altogether.

"Very good, John," Old Man Sheesley said through a smile as he rose and joined Zippy at the map wall. "The map says six people will find the final piece to the map."

"Do you think we're the six people?" asked Jaq.

"Perhaps."

"What's this gold river marked here?" Zippy asked, moving to another section of the map.

"You don't miss much, do you?" Old Man Sheesley replied, looking at Zippy proudly.

"Maybe it's the waterfall in Goldstream Park," Zippy said, looking up at Old Man Sheesley.

"On Woodbury Island?" Gary asked, joining them.

"Yes. That's what it means. Very good! You kids are smarter than I thought, but again, we must not forget the letter."

"What if the letter is a fake?"

"I spent ten years of my life thinking the very same thing, wasting days on Woodbury Island, but I assure you, the letter is real, and not a fake. See for yourself! Does it look like a fake to you?" Old Man Sheesley said, holding the letter out for inspection.

We gathered around it, and Zippy moved in for a closer look with the magnifying glass.

∞ ∞ ∞ ∞ ∞ ∞ ∞

Crushed by the news, we left Old Man Sheesley's house with our heads hanging low. Walking across the lawn to our bikes, we did not say much to each other. I kept going over what Old Man Sheesley had told us about life and about being happy, but I felt I was missing something. Something was nagging at me. Was it my subconscious mind, asking deep questions about my choices in life? Was it my ego, which did not want to give up the search for buried treasure so easily? I did not know, but I was too tired to figure it out tonight. My thoughts were drifting away to my pillow, which peacefully awaited my return.

"All right. If nobody's going to say it, I will," Zippy said, breaking our silence.

"Say what?" Jaq inquired as she pulled her bike from the bushes.

"That the old man is off his rocker," Zippy continued. "Did you hear him babble on about all that secret-of-life stuff?"

"Ah, he wasn't so bad," Gary replied.

"Come on, Gary! Don't tell me you believe the old geezer in there?"

"I'm agreeing with you," Gary replied. "The guy gives me the jeebies, but I don't think he was lying to us."

"Yeah, Zip. It sure sounded like some good advice," I said, responding to the expressions on their faces. "And what about the letter?"

"You mean the letter he wouldn't let us look at for more than a few seconds?" Zippy was more serious than I had ever seen him before.

"I know you want this to be real, Zippy, but you heard the guy, you saw the letter and you saw the map," Jimmy said.

"I'm going. With or without you, I'm still going," Zippy declared.

"Going where?" Gary asked.

"Woodbury Island. If this thing's a hoax, then I need to see it for myself."

"See what?"

"That map led to a cave behind the falls in Goldstream Park."

"There was no cave on our map," Jimmy said.

"That's right, but with the addition of the other two pieces, I saw a cave. I'm telling you. I was just testing him when I asked about the six figures standing on the hill. I didn't want to let him know that I saw the entrance to a cave. Come on, you guys! Trust me. I know what I saw."

"You think the final map is buried inside the cave?" Gary asked, getting on board with Zippy. "What about the whole key thing?"

"I think the keys lead to some treasure—the boat, the house, the carriage—but the maps, found inside each one of those treasures, is what this is about. It's a treasure within a treasure. We have to look past the keys and concentrate on the map, you guys. That's the real deal."

"How can you be sure?" Gary asked.

"Only one way to find out!" Zippy smiled. "What time's the first ferry leave for Woodbury?"

"Not until eight," I answered. "But—"

"But what?" Jaq said, turning to me.

"But the Kaplan Cargo ships sail every morning at four o'clock."

I knew this because our dad would drag us out of bed for opening day of halibut season every year. We could not miss the thundering engines of the big cargo ships leaving the docks at four in the morning. It was like the call of the wild for fisherman.

"Then it's all set. We leave in the morning."

"Wait a second! What's all set?" Jimmy asked.

"What about our game tomorrow at five o'clock?" I asked, agreeing with Jimmy.

"Yeah, and the Fourth of July picnic after that?" Jimmy said. "Do you really want to miss out on all that barbecue and the fireworks show to go search for something on a hunch? Fine. Great. Okay, you want to go over there, cool. I'm with you, but can't we go on Sunday when there's not so much going on? I'm tired, man."

"Sunday might be too late. It's now or never. And Scooter, don't you worry. We'll be back in plenty of time for the game, okay? So we'll meet in front of Hopper's Doughnut Shack at three."

"As in three in the morning?" Jimmy complained. "It's almost eleven now."

"Then you'd better get on home for some beauty sleep, Sunshine," Zippy joked as he pushed down on his pedals and started along the trail for home.

Following him out, we hit the street and split up, drifting through the darkness like bats in the dead of night. I was not sure I would be able to fall asleep. Even though I had enjoyed the advice from Old Man Sheesley, I was excited about the potential discovery of a secret cave in Goldstream Park. Little did I know, however, that tomorrow was the day I would stare into the eyes of death and have to make a decision that would change my life forever.

TREASURE TIP

Listen to your instincts.
They will guide you towards the truth.

21

STOWAWAYS

I was not sure what was more difficult: waking up at 2:30 in the morning or going to sleep at 11:30 at night, knowing you had to wake up in three hours. My Superman sheets never felt so good. I was tired, but it was a good tired. It was the kind of tired that was almost as good as a bowl of my mom's homemade ice cream. Almost.

It was Gary's idea to stuff the alarm clock under my pillow so it would not wake up Mom and Dad. When the first bell rattled my pillow, I knew I would never become a fireman when I got older. Those guys had to wake up, get dressed, and be on the truck in a matter of two minutes. I was a bit slower in my waking process, and that was okay by me. I was good at other things.

Hearing the rustling sounds of our preparations, Peaches nosed her way through the crack of our bedroom door with her tail wagging, as if to ask, "Where we going, boys?" She panted from the excitement and then gave up her belly for a morning rub. We knew if we did not oblige the belly rub request, she would become more rambunctious than she already was, so we both knelt down and rubbed her soft fur. I'm not sure if it was the pressure of petting her belly or that she just felt really comfortable, but something began to attack our noses. It was an awful smell.

"Oh man, she farted!" Gary said in a loud whisper.

The smell was like a stink bomb, rapidly drifting through our room like a skillet of burnt eggs. She popped to her feet, thinking it was playtime because of our stifled laughter, and dropped to her front paws. Peaches would get this wild look on her face and we both knew what that meant. She was ready to bolt around the room, practically daring us to chase her. Thinking fast, Gary grabbed a rawhide bone that had found its way into our toy trunk and tossed it to her. She grabbed the bone and exited to her favorite spot on the living room shag carpet.

Leaving me with the stench of the dog fart, which was always more powerful than any human fart could ever be, Gary tiptoed into the kitchen to make sandwiches while I loaded the backpack for our adventure.

Like a whiz, Gary wrote a note to our parents to explain why we were not in our beds. Normally, when we left before sunrise to go fishing, we'd tell them the location of our fishing trip, but today would be different. Since this

would be a lie, we had to make sure the note was vague
enough to divert any parental suspicions.

Gone fishing. Back later.
—Gary & Scott

With sleep still in our eyes, we met the others outside
of Hopper's Doughnut Shack as planned. As usual, Jimmy
was the last to arrive. His eyes were puffy, and I could tell
he was not happy, because the left side of his face still had
pillow marks like the racing stripes of a stock car. However,
there was no time to make fun of him. We were on a secret
mission and had to press on.

The streets were empty except for a stray dog digging
into an overturned trash can, looking for his morning
breakfast. It was an odd feeling, being on the empty streets.
There was no hustle and bustle of traffic. No horns honking
or people talking—just the eerie quiet of morning, which
was somehow comforting. It was as though danger was far
away. Little did I know, danger was near, and there was
nothing we could do to divert it. We were on a collision
course with it.

We rode down to the commercial docks, locked our
bikes to the bike racks in front of Akili's Arcade, and made
our way onto the loading docks of Kaplan's Shipping
yard. Kaplan Shipping was the largest cargo line around,
and it served all the ports along the Puget Sound. As
crane operators lifted giant containers onto the deck of
the mammoth ship, we slipped past the dozing security
guard, up the large loading ramps and into the belly of
the ship.

The boat ride over to Woodbury's inner harbor would
take over an hour, so we all found a safe hiding spot

between two containers for some much needed shuteye. I think Jimmy was sleeping before his head hit the rolled up jacket he'd brought, which was sure to leave even more sleep lines on that pudgy face of his. As I closed my eyes, I watched a single fishing boat leave the harbor to get an early start on the day's catch. We were tired, and yesterday had been a long day, but a new day was approaching and sleep would do us good.

An hour and a half had raced by in what seemed like only ten minutes. Though drowsy from being jolted awake by the powerful engines, which shook the massive deck as the ship prepared to dock, I felt refreshed from my catnap. The sky was filled with a rainbow of colors. It was a humbling sight of beauty, and I wondered why, in the quiet moments of morning, life seemed simpler than when it was in full swing during the day.

Without talking, for fear of being discovered, we got to our feet and were poised for a clean escape. When the coast was clear, we quickly moved through the labyrinth maze of containers and raced down the giant gangplank to the shipyards of Woodbury Island, Washington.

Gary suggested we step into a local diner for some hot chocolate so we could look over the trail map Zippy had brought from home. Zippy was the kind of guy you wanted with you on an adventure, because he was like an Eagle Scout. Though he was entirely too mischievous to ever be a Boy Scout, the guy was always prepared.

It was now six in the morning, and the diner was crowded with dockworkers and fishermen. I imagined this was the kind of place our dad would frequent when he moved through the Puget Sound, catching king salmon.

Climbing into the corner booth of the small diner, we spread out the map and started the game-planning session.

A few seconds later, an overweight man crossed towards us from behind the counter. He was well into his fifties, and from the looks of the greasy apron tied around his potbelly, he undoubtedly doubled as the fry cook.

"What ya havin'?" he asked in a husky voice.

"Five hot chocolates, please."

"No hot chocolate. Coffee."

"Tea?"

"No tea. Coffee," he said, looking down at us as he leaned forward, pressing his knuckles into the table.

Looking up at his gruff face, we were momentarily speechless.

"Do you have coffee?" Zippy asked in jest, but the man was in no mood for any of our shenanigans.

"He's kidding. Five hot chocolates … I mean five coffees will be fine," Gary said with a fake smile.

"Damn kids," he muttered as he lumbered away and returned with a pot of coffee and five mugs.

"Pour it yourself," he said, grumbling his way back to work.

As Jaq poured the coffee, Zippy began to make sense of the many lines and grids of the trail map.

"Hand me the cream, would ya, Zip?" Jimmy asked.

Looking up from the map, Zippy passed the cream to Jimmy.

"Okay, I looked at the map last night before I went to bed—"

"Sugar?" Jimmy asked, cutting him off again.

Zippy passed him the sugar and waited to see if there would be anything else from Jimmy.

"All set there, Pumpkin?" he asked.

"Yes, thank you," Jimmy replied as he sipped his sugary coffee.

Taking a sip, I noticed the coffee tasted bitter and burnt. Jimmy, forever the sweet tooth, was onto something, so we all quickly doctored the coffee with cream and sugar, which helped it go down much smoother. A warm sugary drink was just what our bodies needed to offset the bone-chilling boat ride.

"The trail head starts just north of town ... here!" Zippy said, indicating a spot on the map. "Looks like about a two-hour hike over to the falls."

"What's that there? A bridge?" I asked, chugging the rest of my coffee.

"Yeah, I don't know. It's red."

"What do you mean, 'it's red'?"

"Red means it's not in use. In-use trails are colored green. Here, and here," Zippy answered. "We'll have to see once we get there, but I think this will get us there the quickest. You guys ready?"

Exiting the diner, I felt the buzz of excitement running through me. This was going to be a great time, I thought, but when I noticed how fast Jimmy was talking about the boat ride, I knew I was feeling more than the anticipation of the adventure. Something was happening inside of me. Jimmy started talking even faster, if that was possible.

"What if we get lost? I mean, I don't want to get lost, but we should have a game plan in case anyone does get lost. You know, gets separated from the group. Falls behind. You know ... that sort of thing. Some kind of sign, because stuff like that happens ... you know, getting lost ... when you have this many people on a hike. You know?"

"Hey, slow down, Jimmy," I finally said, interrupting his rant.

"What?" Jimmy asked, spinning around to face me.

"You're talking too fast."

"I'm not talking too fast. You're talking too fast," Jimmy said, chattering away.

"You're both talking too fast, and it's startin' to freak me out," Gary said.

"What's freakin' you out?" Jaq quickly asked, joining our rapid-fire discussion.

"He's freakin' me out," Gary answered, indicating Jimmy.

"I'm freakin' you out? He's freakin' me out," Jimmy said, looking at me with eyes wide, like two jelly-filled doughnuts. "Stop moving your eyebrows like that, man."

"What are you talking about?" Gary replied.

"Scooter's eyebrows. He looks like Bugs Bunny, and it's wiggin' me out."

"Wiggin' you out? What the heck's that mean?" Zippy inquired, getting excited from all the commotion.

"Okay, now you're all starting to wig me out," I finally said.

"Oh my god, he does look like Bugs Bunny!" Gary added.

What was happening? My heart was like a funny car ripping down a drag strip, and everyone was looking at me and laughing. Not really at my eyebrows, but the uncontrollable zing that had entered our bodies, courtesy of the coffee, which was a first for everyone.

"My heart! It's going to pop. It's beating so fast—" Jimmy said, clutching his chest.

"Mine, too," Jaq said, becoming worried, but laughing just the same. She suddenly backed away as paranoia began to overtake her, because she couldn't stop laughing.

"I'm getting dizzy," Zippy yelled through a snort.

"All right. Hold on!" Gary said, reeling us in. "Everyone just take a deep breath and calm down."

After a few more chuckles, we finally took a deep breath. We were eager to try anything that might make the uncomfortable feeling go away, but it did not. When we took a second deep breath, Zippy kept looking at me. He had a strange look on his face.

"What?" I finally asked.

"Your eyebrows! Oh man, they do make you look like Bugs Bunny!"

Before we knew it, we were all laughing again, but this time there was no holding back. It was the side-aching laughter that made you snort through your nose for air. And we did, but when Jimmy did, a chunk of snot shot out of his nose like a bullet, which only made us laugh even harder.

TREASURE TIP

Friendships are memories. Make them often.

22

RUNNING LIKE THE WIND

The early morning fog drifted through the dense trees as though somebody had set off a whole bag of smoke bombs. The sweet smell of evergreens filled the air, which reminded me of home. Fallen branches and needles crunched under our feet as we walked single file along the narrow trail.

The effects of the coffee had finally worn off, and we were now well over an hour into the hike. Stopping to the side of the trail, I leaned against Jaq so I could dislodge a small pebble from my Wallabee walking boot. The

Wallabee was my all-time favorite shoe, even when I was not hiking. The soft, gummy-like sole made me feel like I was walking on air. And if I ever had to run, the shoes had a way of making me feel like I was running faster than I actually was.

"Let's go, you two," Gary yelled back to us. "We don't have all day!"

"Lay off, man. I got a pebble in my Wallabees," I yelled back as I tipped my boot upside down to dislodge the stone.

"Are those Wallabees really all that comfortable?" Jaq inquired as I laced up my boot.

"Best pair of shoes I own. It's like wearing slippers, but you can run in them too. Why?"

"I don't know. I was kind of thinkin' about gettin' me a pair," she replied as we caught up to the others.

"Yeah, probably not a good idea."

"Why? Cool enough for you, cool enough for me."

"Yeah, but Jaq … they're for guys."

"You think I care about that? *Function over fashion.* That's my motto."

"Which is why the girls at school are always giving you grief."

"You think I care what Brandy Larson thinks about my shoes?"

"Quiet!" Jimmy announced, breaking into our conversation. "I think I heard something."

Everybody stopped to listen, but we heard nothing.

"Quit playing around, Jimmy," Zippy snapped from the front of the line.

"I'm not. I heard something back there."

"There's something you're going to have to learn, Jimmy. This is the forest. It's not Water Street. It's not the playground at school. Animals and creatures of all kinds live here, and we're just visitors. You're going to hear things, see things—

"—BEAR!" Zippy's face turned white as he shouted at us.

"All right, you don't have to yell at me."

"BEAR!" Zippy said, frozen in his tracks.

"We heard you," I replied.

"NO! BEAR!" Zippy shouted again.

He spun around and began to run. I turned and looked back down the trail and saw a black bear running towards us, full tilt.

"BEAR!" I yelled.

I grabbed Jaq's arm and we all took off after Zippy. Jimmy was the last to turn and see the bear, but he just stood there, crippled with fear.

"BEAR!" He finally repeated the warning and took off after us like an Olympic sprinter. Jimmy was a pudgy kid who could barely make a base hit out of what normally would be a double for the rest of us, but not today. He was bookin' past us so fast that he was a blur. We all knew how lazy he was, but seeing him run from that bear, I realized he was simply suffering from under-achiever-itis. This kid could flat out run!

The trees were racing past us like the tunnels of the Matterhorn ride at Disneyland. Jimmy caught up to me, passed me, then passed Gary and Jaq. He even passed Zippy, who was the fastest of all of us. I was now in last place, which was a bad thing. When I looked back and saw the bear gaining on me, my heart skipped more than a few beats. My feet were pounding the trail, and I'm sure we all were running faster than we had ever run before.

The bear was so close that I could hear the thundering sounds of his massive paws. Then suddenly, a rifle shot rang out. We all hit the deck, and I heard the bear fall to the ground right behind me.

"What the heck was that?" Jimmy said scrambling to his feet.

I turned around and saw the black bear on the ground, writhing in pain, trying to stand up. He was dying, but he still had plenty of fight left in him. As he rose to his feet again, a second shot rang out. This time the bear fell to the ground with a giant *THUD!* He was struggling for air. Jaq grabbed my arm, frightened by what she saw.

"Scooter! What's happening? What's going on?" she asked as tears began to fall down her face.

"Hunters," Gary said, directing our attention towards two hunters appearing through the drifting fog. They moved quickly from the hillside above us and carried large, high-powered rifles. From what I could tell, these guys were professional hunters, whatever that meant.

"Great shot there, Dave!" the older man said. His voice echoed through the forest.

"Couldn't have done it without your help, Todd. If you hadn't cut him off when you did, I would never have been able to make that shot," said the other man as they drew closer. "Looks like a keeper. Must be close to 300 pounds."

I gazed at the fallen bear. He was dying right before our eyes. His giant chest heaved in and out, struggling for the life that was being ripped from him faster than he could breathe it in. His eyes seemed to look right through me, asking me why this had happened. I didn't know I was crying until I felt the warm tears running down my face.

The younger hunter, who I assumed was Dave, arrived at his kill. He set down his rifle and, without pausing for a second, drew a large Buck Knife from a sheath on his belt and slit the throat of the bear like Jack the Ripper. The bear's head fell to the ground with a morbid thump. Thick red blood, redder than I had ever known blood to be, began to stain the ground below his massive bear body.

There would be no more breaths of life for the animal. There would be no more hunting for berries. No more searching for honey. No more naps in the summer sun, no more playing with cubs and no more winter hibernation. It was over. The bear was dead.

"Why did you do that?" I asked, looking up at the man.

He was about my father's age, but his eyes where much thinner than my father's. This man had the eyes of a killer.

"Well, son, you don't want that blood to settle into the meat," he said as if he was teaching me something, the way a father teaches a son.

But this man was not my father, and I was not his son. I did not want to know anything about hunting and swore that from that moment on, I would never pick up a gun to hunt any animal. Ever.

"You didn't have to shoot him," Jaq said, crying.

"Well, little girl, if we hadn't, he would've caught up and killed you," the older hunter said.

"He wasn't running after us. He was running from you!" Zippy snapped.

"Either way, I'd say it's your lucky day. You should be thanking us."

"What are you kids doing up here, anyway?" asked the hunter who had killed the bear.

"We could ask you the same question," Zippy retorted. "This is a national park."

"Well, I'll be! I'm guessin' you're right about that, but up there—atop that ridge—huntin' ain't against the law."

"You killed him on protected land. *That's* against the law," Gary said.

"But we wounded him well within the range."

"You didn't wound him. He was fine, running right there behind us. He was fine."

Before we could say another word, the hunter raised his rifle and suddenly shot the bear in his hind leg. "See there. That's the shot that wounded him," he said with a laugh.

I could not believe what I had just seen. We were all shocked into silence. There was no more debate. The bear was dead.

"Are you going to eat him?" Gary asked, which was kind of an odd question from my brother.

"You betcha. Eat him and put that big head of his right onto the wall of my den. Yeah, going to look great with the pool table, huh, Todd?"

The two men were like immature kids the way they laughed back and forth together at the expense of a dead bear.

"What?" Jaq said, rising to her feet as if she was about to rush the man.

"What do you mean, *what*? This here bear's my trophy."

"Your trophy? Your trophy?" Jaq was becoming unglued.

"I think it's time you kids be on your way. Unless you want to see Dave here cut the bear's heart out."

"WHAT?" we all shouted in unison.

Upon hearing what was next in this already horrifying experience, we all got to our feet and hurried away. It was one of the saddest things I had ever seen. I did not understand why men needed to shoot animals so they could put them on their walls as trophies. Hunting to put food on your family's table is one thing—but to kill for sport? For the kicks of it? That I did not get.

"I hope someone shoots you one day!" Jaq fired back at the two men.

"Well, good thing hunting kids is against the law, little girl. Otherwise, you and that smart mouth of yours would be in a world of hurt."

Jaq was not afraid. She wanted to do something, but there was nothing we could do. The bear was dead, and those men had guns. It was time for us to go.

"Come on, Jaq," I said, putting an arm around her. "Let's go."

The experience was hard on her, not so much because she was the only girl, but because she really cared about animals, and no one should have to watch one die that way. I had seen violence in the movies and even the news on television, but this was different. It was right there in front of me, and it would forever change the way I felt about animals. I did not understand why some things lived, while others had to die.

I was only thirteen years old, but I knew the bear had not done anything wrong. Nothing deserved to die like that. The bear had not killed a rancher's cattle. He had not wandered into town and wreaked havoc on the town's people. He was just being a bear, minding his own bear business, when *BOOM!* Two knucklehead hunters had come along and killed him. It was not right.

Forty-five minutes had passed since the bear incident, and I had fallen back from the others. Nobody seemed to notice, however. I guess walking in silence was in honor of the fallen bear. After a few minutes, Jaq fell back and walked beside me.

"Hey Scott?" she said meekly. "Is something wrong with me?"

"What do you mean?"

"I don't know. The girls at school, they … they treat me like some kind of outcast sometimes."

"Jaq. Come on. You're the coolest girl I know.

"Cooler than Brandy Larson?"

"What? No. Well, she's different."

"She's stuck-up," Jaq shot back, looking straight at me.

"Who are we talking about? Her or you?"

"Me, I guess. I just don't understand why the girls all treat me ... so ... you know ... different."

"Because, you are kind of different.

"Different how?

"Well, you hang out with us, for one. That makes you *really* different," I answered with a laugh, trying to lighten her spirits.

"No. Come on. I'm serious."

"Jaq, I don't know. I guess you being a tomboy makes them feel, you know, threatened."

"What do you mean, I'm a tomboy?"

"Jaq, you can throw a baseball better than any guy I know. And you dress—"

"What's wrong with the way I dress?"

"What? Um ... forget it. It's nothing."

"Don't do that. You wouldn't say something if it was nothing. Now, what is it?"

"Maybe if you dressed the way the girls do, they might—"

"What, like wear a dress?" she asked. "You shouldn't judge a person by what they wear."

"Well, girls aren't like that, especially those girls," I replied, not sure how to get myself out of this conversation. "You've seen Brandy. The feathered hair. The girlie clothes. She's ... perfect."

"Is that why you like her?"

"Jaq, stop!" I finally said.

"Over there!" Zippy announced from the lead.

Jimmy started running to catch up to Gary and Zippy.

"Let's go! Hurry it up, you two," Gary said, looking back towards us.

"Would you hold your horses already! We're coming," I yelled before I stepped in front of Jaq. "Hey! You okay?"

"Oh yeah, just making conversation ... you know. No biggie," she replied, brushing past me to catch up with the others.

But I knew it was more than a "no biggie" thing for her. She felt like an outsider in her own skin, and all she wanted to do was fit in with the other girls at school. I understood what she was going through more than I cared to admit. I was shorter than everyone else. I was younger than everyone else in my grade. And when it came to sports, I was marginal at best. But what could I do about it? I guess that was part of growing up: learning to accept the things you cannot change and work for things you can. I was just happy to be away from those hunters.

As my thoughts cleared, I started up the trail to join the others. With every step, I began to hear a noise grow louder in the distance. It was a low rumbling, which made me want to stop dead in my tracks. Suddenly, I could feel the earth move under my feet, but what was it? Why was everyone just standing around? Was another black bear closing in on them for the kill?

I was too afraid to turn around and see if the sound was coming from behind me, so I started running towards the others as fast as I could.

TREASURE TIP

What other people think of you is none of your business.

23

A BRIDGE TOO FAR

With every step I took towards my friends, the strange rumbling transformed into a massive, earthshaking thunder. Joining them on the ridge, I saw one of the most amazing sights I had ever seen in my short thirteen years of life.

We were standing before a giant river gorge that cut into the earth at least two hundred feet down. The water slammed against the jagged rocks below with immense force. It was impossible to judge how fast the river was flowing. It was at this point I realized this was the same river we had seen on the map back in Old Man Sheesley's hideout. A small part of me wished he could be here to see what we were seeing. It was magnificent, to say the least.

Scanning the river, my gaze turned upward to the giant falls, which had been responsible for creating the impressive canyon before us. Sheets of water shot out from the top of the waterfall, creating a heavy mist that fell in slow motion to the rushing water below.

"How the heck are we going to get all the way down there?" Jaq said, staring down at the river.

"Zippy?" Gary looked at him. "Why don't you give the map a look-see and show us the way?"

"There!" Jimmy blurted out, pointing to a rope bridge that stretched across the canyon, some ninety-five feet in length.

"What good's that going to do us?" I asked. "Get us to the other side?"

"You got a better idea?"

As I found myself on the brink of a back and forth with Jimmy, I wondered why Zippy was so quiet. Usually he was counterpoint to Jimmy's every point, but right now he remained quiet.

"Zip?" Gary asked. "The map?"

Zippy finally knelt down, unzipped his backpack and opened the trail map. We watched as his finger traced the trail route and his head popped up to scan the area around us. After a few seconds, he turned the map ninety degrees, scanned our surroundings again and looked back down at the map.

"What's wrong?" I asked.

"We missed the turn."

"What do you mean, we missed the turn?" Jimmy asked quickly. "We never left the trail."

"Relax, man. I made a mistake. We're off course, okay?"

"How far off course?" Gary asked.

"A ways. We ran past the fork in the trail back when the bear chased us—we should've turned right, which would've led us down river. See here?" Zippy said, pointing to a section of the map.

It would be nice to say that we could find a way down from this side of the river, but we were standing on the edge of a cliff.

"Check from the other side, Zippy," Jimmy said. "Maybe if we cross the bridge we'll find another way down."

Zippy scanned the map again and found a small dotted trail on the other side of the canyon. "Yeah, there's a trail, but it's dotted in red, which means it's abandoned. I think we should go back and start over."

"We don't have time to go back," Jimmy said. "Let's go across the bridge and at least give it a try."

"Hold on, man. We don't know if the trail's even still there," Zippy replied.

"There's only one way to find out," Jimmy said with a smile.

"Hup ho, Jimmy!" Gary said, looking at the rest of us. "Look who's suddenly found nerves of steel."

"What?" Jimmy asked.

"He's right, man. That bear changed you," I added.

"What are you talking about?"

"Jimmy, I've never seen you run so fast. Well, there was that one time—"

"—when Ms. Goodwin's dog chased us out of her yard," Jaq said, finishing my sentence.

"Exactly," we said in unison.

"Well, I sure wasn't about to let some bear take a bite out of my butt," Jimmy said with a laugh. "Come on, you guys. Let's give it a try."

"If only we could find a bear to chase him down the first base line during tonight's game, we might be onto something, eh, Gary?" Zippy joked.

"Why you gotta be such a cool breeze all the time?" Jimmy snapped.

"Oh, come on. I'm just playin' with ya, Flash Gordon," Zippy said, folding the map.

"No, you're being a jerk and makin' fun of me, and I'm getting tired of it. Now are we going do this thing or what?"

Jimmy was angry, and he did not wait for an answer. He disappeared into the trees towards the rope bridge. His walk was more confident than I had ever seen it before. We all just looked at each other, astonished.

"Guess he told you," Gary said to Zippy as we started after him.

"Guess he did," Zippy replied, slinging his backpack over his shoulder.

As we drew closer to the rope bridge, Jimmy's idea of going across seemed less and less likely, because the bridge was dilapidated and older than any of us cared to even think about. The mere thought of walking across it sent a chill through my veins. Today would not be a good day to die.

Large sections of the wooden planks making up the floor of the bridge were cracked, and in some places, entire planks were missing. If that was not bad enough, the rope handrails looked weathered and frayed, and there was a big sign in the center of the trail: "Foot Bridge Closed!"

"Yeah, I am not going across that thing," Jaq said.

"Looks pretty old," Gary added.

"What about you, Superman? You ready to bust out that cape of yours and show us the way?" Zippy said, looking for laughs from the rest of us.

Without warning, Jimmy tackled Zippy to the ground. Everybody had a breaking point, and I guess Jimmy had reached his. Gary quickly grabbed Jimmy's leg and pulled him off of Zippy, who was pivoting on top of his backpack like an overturned turtle.

"Knock it off!" Gary ordered.

"Yeah, you idiot! What, are you out of your mind?" Zippy screamed, struggling to get up.

"I'm talking to the both of you!"

"He's the one who jumped me!" Zippy said in defense.

"Yeah, and you deserved it," Gary snapped. "Now, shut up—both of you!"

Jimmy got to his feet and brushed himself off.

"I figure we got two choices here, and we certainly don't have time for horsin' around by you two!" Gary ordered.

"What are the choices?" Jaq asked.

Gary paused for a second, and I recognized the look that came over his face. It was a look my older brother would get when he was working things out. His eyes shot upward as if the answers were stored in the upper left portion of his brain. With a slight nod indicating he had found what he was looking for, he scanned the terrain before us.

"Okay. Three choices, actually. We could double back and waste another two hours to get back on course, which would make us miss the ferry, not to mention our baseball game ..."

"Not an option," I said. "What's next?"

"We could head towards the falls and hopefully find a way down."

"Or?" I asked again, because neither of these options sounded attractive. Sure, I wanted to find the treasure, but I did not want to miss the baseball game. Tommy was not going to get off that easy, and I wanted to see Brandy Larson's face when I cracked a home run off of her boyfriend.

"Or ... we can—" Gary turned his gaze to the rope bridge, but before he could finish his sentence, he saw Jimmy already three steps along the rickety construction.

"Jimmy!"

"What are you doing?"

"Hey man! I'm sorry. You don't have to prove anything, Jimmy!" Zippy said, climbing to his feet.

"You think I'm doing this to prove something to you? Don't make me laugh," Jimmy fired back as he continued across the bridge.

"Guess he told you," Gary said with a chuckle. "Again."

"Shut up, Gary," Zippy snarled.

Following Jimmy, we started out single file, with ten feet between us. Zippy was behind Jimmy. Gary went next, followed by Jaq. I decided to go last, not because I was scared, but because—okay, I was a little scared, but I did not let on about that. The truth was, I was not fond of heights. I would not say I was afraid of heights. I just did not like 'em. Then it occurred to me that going last was probably the worst thing I could do. If there were any stress cracks in the small, decaying two-by-six wooden planks below our feet, the weight of the others ahead of me would push the boards to the brink of breaking, if they had not broken already. But I could not think about that right now. What I needed to focus on was my feet moving across that bridge, because I was already falling behind.

As I stepped onto the bridge, I could hear one of the boards creak under my weight. I stepped forward and transferred all my weight to the next creaking board. Suddenly, my foot shot through and landed on the rocks at the side of the canyon. This was not a good way to start, I thought.

"You okay back there?" Gary yelled back when he heard the boards break.

"Yeah. Fine. Great."

I was replying more to myself than anyone else, but I was not great. I was not great at all. I was anything *but* great. I kept moving anyway, and before I knew it, I was in the center of the bridge. This was not so bad. No sweat. Then, just as my thoughts began to reassure me that everything would be okay, the rope bridge lurched to my left and began to swing back and forth. At the same moment, I heard Zippy let out a scream.

Looking past the others, I saw that Zippy's foot had broken through a board just the way mine had. The only difference was he was dangling over a two hundred-foot drop to the canyon below. Like the jaws of an angry alligator, the jagged rocks surrounding the rushing river were waiting for him to fall. If he did fall, he would surely die, because nobody—and I mean nobody—could survive a fall like that, rocks or no rocks. We were just too high.

"Help!" Zippy screamed. His legs were flailing under the deck of the bridge while he desperately clung to the rope with both hands. He was panicking, which made the situation even worse than it already was.

"Stop kicking!" Gary ordered in a grim voice.

Zippy's struggle was making the rope bridge start to swing back and forth.

"Give me your hand!" Jimmy said as he dropped to his knees. He laid his belly across the wooden planks and reached out for Zippy.

"I can't!" Zippy cried out.

"Come on, man. You can do it. Just let go with one hand and grab my hand."

"You aren't strong enough to pull me up!" Zippy yelled, losing his grip.

"I won't drop you. I promise," Jimmy said with calming eyes.

Zippy stopped struggling long enough to look up to his unlikely savior. He grabbed hold of Jimmy's hand, but his weight was too much. Jimmy's body lurched forward. It looked like he was being pulled into a pit of quicksand, and there was no escape.

"Kick your legs up!" Gary ordered.

"I can't."

"Kick up your legs!" Jimmy screamed.

"I can't!"

"You're going to kill us both!"

The mounting commotion made the rope bridge swing back and forth more violently. It was as though we were in the web of an angry spider. I did not want to face what was about to happen. I was about to watch my friend die.

24

THE GREAT FALL(S)

The old rope bridge was like a carnival ride gone terribly wrong, and I wanted to get off. Unable to move forward or backward, all I could do was hold on for dear life. That life, however, seemed like it was being ripped away from me without permission. There was nothing I could do. There was nothing any of us could do.

The swinging motion of the bridge was now gaining momentum like the arm of a grandfather clock. *Tick tock ... tick tock.* Then suddenly, the momentum began to work in our favor. With the bridge swinging back and forth,

Zippy's legs were like the end of a bullwhip, snapping upward with every swing. If only he could kick his legs up far enough, he would be able to grab hold of the deck ropes where Jimmy was lying.

The idea sounded good, but the commotion was causing Jimmy to slide into the gaping pit of danger. Thinking fast, he spread his legs out, searching for anything his feet might hold onto. On the next swing, the momentum on the bridge and Zippy's adrenalin-charged kicks flipped his body up and over the deck rope like a rag doll, slamming him down hard on Jimmy like one of those fake wrestlers on late-night television. I could hear the wooden slats crack from their combined weight, but the jolt seemed to slow down the swinging motion of the bridge. We could finally breathe a sigh of relief. We were going to be okay. We were all going to get out of this situation alive.

The celebration, however, was short-lived as the handrail rope in my left hand suddenly went slack. My head spun around, and to my growing horror, I saw the handrail rope, which was fastened to a metal post at the canyon's edge, beginning to fray. My vision was like the zoom of a movie camera, shooting rapidly to a close-up of the fraying rope. Fear was not moving through my body anymore—my entire being was fear! I was enveloped in it and could not see my way out.

"The rope is breaking!" I screamed to the others.

Their voices wailed in response as the rope slacked even more.

"Jaq, keep moving!" I screamed again. "Go! Go! Go! We gotta go!"

"I can't move my feet!" she said.

Then somehow she broke free from her prison of fear and looked as if she was in a wild game of hopscotch, the way her feet shot past the pit of danger below. One step ... two. Hop! Jump! The light stepping motion seemed to work, so I followed her, step for step. One step ... two. Hop! Jump! Repeat.

Just as I reached for Gary's outstretched hand of safety, the handrail rope finally broke and started to collapse into the canyon below. I dove for my brother's hand. He pulled me to the side just as the rope bridge swung upward and fell over onto itself. We froze in disbelief. The platform we had been walking on only seconds ago was now upside down. If anyone had been on the bridge, they would be dead.

Standing in silence, we all knew what had just happened. We had cheated death, and it was not something we could just chalk up to one of our many adventures, the way we often did. When you're my age, you think you are going to live forever. You think you are invincible ... until something like this happens. My dad used to say that moments like this, when you are pushed beyond the limit of what you think is possible, either make you or break you. They make you see things more clearly than ever before, and at this moment, to my eyes, everything was crystal clear.

Staring out over the jaws of death, Zippy put his hand on Jimmy's shoulder. "Thanks for coming back for me, Jimmy. You saved my life, and hey, I promise not to make fun of you ever again."

Jimmy slowly turned to look Zippy in the eye. "We get out of here, our friendship ... it's over!"

Jimmy shrugged Zippy's hand from his shoulder and walked away.

"Come on, man. Don't be like that. I'm serious," Zippy replied.

Jimmy turned towards him in defiance. "So am I."

"What did I do?"

"It's not what you did. It's who you are, and if it takes me saving your life for you to respect me, then you're no friend of mine. In fact, you know what? You were never my friend. You were just someone I put up with."

Sometimes we'd say things to each other we did not mean, but I think Jimmy meant every word just then. He had finally had enough.

After making our way down the precarious rocky trail, we found ourselves standing before the majestic Goldstream Falls. The sound was deafening, yet peaceful. I often wondered what it was about water and why it brought so much peace to my life. Whether it was in the form of the ocean, a calm lake, a river, a stream or a thundering waterfall, water somehow spoke to me. Perhaps it was the life that was generated from a body of water. Whatever the reason, when I was around water, I seemed to be happier than when I was not.

"Anybody see a cave?" Zippy yelled, but we saw nothing.

"It's been over forty years since that map was drawn!" I shouted.

"So?" Gary replied.

"So maybe the cave collapsed, or eroded away altogether."

"Look around, man. It's all rock. Rocks don't erode!" Zippy yelled, correcting me.

"What's that?" Jaq asked, pointing at the waterfall.

"I think they call that a waterfall," Jimmy yelled back with a smile.

"No. That!" she said, indicating the edge of the waterfall.

At first it was hard to see what she was talking about, but after staring at the falls a moment longer, we could make out something behind them. As sheets of water fell to the rocky floor beneath our feet, a momentary window opened in the waterfall. Through that window we saw a dark outline. It was the entrance to a cave. We had found it.

We took turns and shot through the sheets of water. The trick was to time it perfectly so you could hit the window of opportunity without getting wet. I guess all those years of dodgeball must have helped, because we all made it through without getting a drop of water on our clothes.

Behind the majestic waterfall was the coolest place I had ever been. It was cooler than any fort we had ever built, and the ultimate in secrecy. We entered the cave, and the beams of our flashlights cut through the murky darkness, which seemed to go on forever. It was more like a mineshaft than a simple cave. The air was cold, and it smelled like an old, musty fish tank.

With every step, our feet sank into the moist floor of the cave the way they did on the playground at school after a heavy rain. We walked deeper and deeper into the endless sea of darkness that stretched on before us. When I looked back, I could no longer see the glow of daylight from the cave's entrance. We were deep inside the earth now, and I felt both excited and afraid because I had never been inside such a large cave. A buzz of anticipation ran through me.

Looking around, I directed my flashlight beam to the ceiling. Railroad ties lined the walls to keep it from collapsing, but they were old and did not look sturdy. My mind began to race with thoughts of what might go wrong. How long ago had the cave been dug, and by whom? Was it an abandoned gold or diamond mine? Was it marked on the trail map? Was it on any map other than the treasure map? Would anyone ever find us if something were to happen?

"Wow, you guys! Check it out," Jimmy said from the darkness ahead of me.

I was finally grateful for Jimmy's nonstop chatter because it caused the uncontrollable thoughts rushing through my mind to subside.

"Shine your lights on the walls," he said.

One by one, our beams of light flashed on the cave walls. Tiny lights flickered like an army of fireflies.

"What the heck is it?" I asked.

"You think it's gold?" Jimmy wondered aloud.

"Gold is gold, Jimmy," Zippy said. "That's why it's called gold. Because it looks like—"

Jimmy shot him a look that made him clarify his statement.

"What? I'm just saying. Those are—"

"—condensation crystals," Jaq said, finishing Zippy's sentence. "You aren't the only A student here, buddy boy. I take notes in class, too."

"I guess she told you," Gary said, amused with another shot towards Zippy.

"Let's keep moving," Zippy said, but not before he shot his light in Gary's eyes in retaliation.

Before we could turn and continue our descent into the cave, we heard the chambering of a gun echo throughout the cave.

"Nobody move a muscle!" the voice growled from the darkness.

TREASURE TRIP

Happiness is not a result of what happens.
Happiness is the cause of how you live each moment.

25

THE BETRAYAL

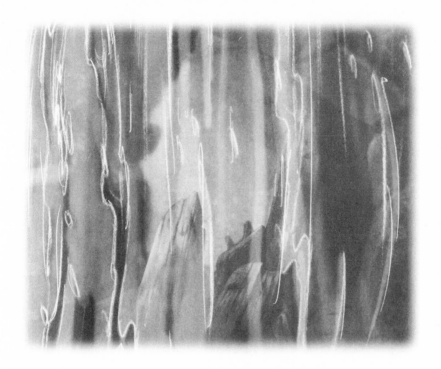

"I guess I underestimated your perseverance."

The voice sounded familiar. My throat tightened. It was as if I was trying to speak, but the words were knotted so tightly in my state of confusion that I almost choked on them.

I could not believe my eyes. Old Man Sheesley was standing in the darkness before us. My flashlight revealed a very large pistol held firmly in his aging hand. The betrayal sank deep, like a knife twisting and turning in my gut. My heart fell into my Wallabees, and there was nothing I could say or do.

"Get that light out of my eyes!" he ordered in a voice that did not fit the image of a frail, old man.

It was the voice of a man who was not only sharp in mind, but strong in body as well. I guess those nightly walks to Aldrich's Pub & Grocery were more for his fitness than to quench his thirst. The man was training his body for a moment like this one.

"Looking for this?" he said with a condescending smile.

His outstretched hand held the fourth and final cylinder of the *Keys of Lafitte* treasure hunt. The metal was corroded and discolored like the one I had found on Tommy's sailboat. Old Man Sheesley had found the final piece of the puzzle.

"A day late and a dollar short, as the saying goes, eh kids?" he said with a laugh. "I have to give you credit, though. You guys didn't give up. That shows a lot of heart, but I'm the one with the map, so I guess heart doesn't matter much now, does it?"

"But the letter?" I asked with my mouth hanging open, locked in disbelief.

"Pretty good diversion, don't you think?"

"Obviously not," Zippy said, breaking his own silence.

"I'll give you that, John. I'll give you that."

"Look, old man, I told you—my name is Zippy!"

"Yes. How could I forget?" Old Man Sheesley said. "You know, of everyone in town, you and your father—"

"Don't you say anything about his father!" Jimmy said, stepping forward in Zippy's defense.

The gesture did not go unnoticed by Zippy. It was hard to imagine that only an hour ago the two were fighting like a couple of angry wombats, wrestling heatedly on the ground.

"Get your fat butt back in line, little man," he growled at Jimmy before turning his attention back to Zippy. "Your father was a good man, Zippy. What happened wasn't fair to him, or you. Nobody should go through life without a father. What I was going to say was, of everyone in town, I knew you were going to be my fiercest competitor."

"Why?" Zippy asked.

"Because fruit doesn't fall far from the tree. Your old man was one of the smartest people in town, but like you, he was one step behind me. Now hand over the map."

"My dad was twice the man you are, you old ... buzzard!"

"I don't disagree, but I'm the one holding all the maps," Old Man Sheesley rumbled. "Now I'm assuming you have the map in your backpack, so hand it over, and I'll be on my way."

"I don't have it."

"Hand it over."

"I don't have it."

Old Man Sheesley raised the gun and pointed it at Zippy. "Give me the map."

Without warning, he fired a shot just over our heads. The blast from the gun was so loud I thought my eardrums had burst. Dirt from the ceiling rained down around us. The echo of the gunshot finally dissipated in the darkness.

"Next time, I won't miss," Old Man Sheesley warned, though I could barely hear him through the ringing in my ears.

"Give it to him, Zip," Gary finally said. "We know where he lives."

"Yes. Yes, you do. Come over any time, and I'll feed you to my dog like all the other runaways."

What? The rumors were true?

"Yeah, that's right. Hand over that map. Now!"

Zippy did not move. His eyes just narrowed and stared back at the old man, despite the fear rushing through him.

Old Man Sheesley walked over to one of the vertical railroad ties supporting the ceiling beam over our heads. Picking up what looked like an old two-by-four board, he wedged it behind the vertical railroad tie.

"What are you doing?" I asked.

But there was no answer. Old Man Sheesley used the two-by-four as a lever, and began to wedge the bottom of the support from its hold in the cave's muddy floor. The ceiling beam over us moved, and small rocks and dirt began to rain down. We backed away, further into the cave.

"Wait!" Zippy yelled when more debris fell before us.

Looking up, Old Man Sheesley stopped prying with the two-by-four. After a brief pause, Zippy dug into his backpack and threw the cylinder at Old Man Sheesley's feet.

"Don't be a sore loser, John," the old man replied as he picked up our cylinder and slid it into an inside jacket pocket.

"Do you think Jacques Pierre Lafitte wanted just anyone to find his great-grandfather's lost treasure? I'm simply smarter than the rest of the people in town. You all sit in front of your televisions every night, wasting life away like a bunch of doped white mice in a college lab."

"So, you lied to us," I said, looking up at him.

"Not entirely, but you should've minded your own business. You're lucky I don't make you pay for breaking my window. But I guess missing your baseball game is punishment enough."

"What?" I said, quickly. "You can't do that."

"Yeah, and who's going to stop me?"

"We'll stop you."

"No, you won't."

"You going to shoot us all?"

"Shoot a child? Now I can do a lot of things in life, but that? No."

"So you're going to let us go?"

"I didn't say that," Old Man Sheesley said. "Now, back away."

"We'll find you!" Jimmy snarled at him.

Without answering, Old Man Sheesley leaned onto the two-by-four, popping the railroad tie from its hold. We dove for cover as the ceiling collapsed and a wall of debris shot towards us. A blanket of terror! We were trapped in the cave with no way out.

26

TRAPPED

My eyes tried to focus through the darkness. The dust was so thick it was hard to tell which way was forward and which was backward. Turning to the left, I found my flashlight glowing under a pile of rock. Aside from the sound of dirt raining down on my backpack, the cave was deathly silent.

"Everyone okay?" I heard Gary say as he coughed the dust from his lungs.

"I'm okay," Zippy's voice answered behind me.

"Me too," Jimmy said, coughing.

"Jaq?" I asked, but there was no answer.

This was no time to panic. Grabbing my flashlight, my eyes followed the beam of light as it struggled to cut through the darkness. Turning to my left, I saw her arm sticking out from a pile of rubble. Jaq was buried alive. I sprang to my feet.

"Over here. She's buried!" I said, digging into the dirt with my hands before I could finish my sentence.

Flashlight beams bounced back and forth as the guys scrambled to help me. Jaq was lying face down, and she wasn't moving.

"Hurry! Turn her over!" Zippy ordered.

The black mud from the floor covered her face. Her eyes were closed. Suddenly, she sputtered and coughed. She was alive.

"Jaq? Are you okay?" I said, kneeling next to her.

"What happened?" she asked, coming to.

"I'm going to kill that old man," I said, more furious than I had ever been.

"You'll have to wait in line," Jaq said, sitting up and wiping the mud from her face. "I'm gonna egg his house something good."

Slowly our flashlights lifted to discover the nightmare before us. The only way out of the cave was now blocked with a wall of rock and debris. The support beams that used to hold the ceiling in place were snapped in half like toothpicks.

"You guys think there's another way out of here?" Jimmy asked, shining his flashlight into the endless darkness behind us.

"We don't have time to look for one," Zippy said, climbing to his feet as he moved towards the rock pile before us.

"Don't be ridiculous," Jimmy replied. "We don't know if the cave collapsed altogether. I say we walk into the cave and see what we can find."

"Yeah? And what do you think you're going to breathe, Einstein?" Zippy said. "The farther down we go, the less oxygen there'll be. This is our only way out."

"I don't know, Zip," Gary started to say. "Jimmy might be right on this one. Even if we dig through, that ceiling could collapse at any moment and bury us alive for good."

"This is the way I came in, and this is the way I'm going out," Zippy said.

Without a moment's hesitation, he started to clear the debris like a dog digging after a juicy bone. After watching for a minute, and seeing the headway he was making, the rest of us exchanged looks back and forth, wondering if we should join him.

"Don't just stand there!" he said, looking back at us. "Give me some light over here."

Jaq held the flashlights as the rest of us passed basketball-sized rocks like a team of firefighters passing buckets of water to fight a fire. About ten minutes later, Zippy reached his hand through to the other side.

"Jaq, give me some light."

Our eyes followed the flashlight beam through the opening. We were going to make it! Clearing a tight crawl space, Zippy inched his body through the hole, head first. Seconds later, he popped his head up from the other side.

"Let's go! Jaq, you're next," he said.

We helped Jaq to the top of the debris pile and watched as Zippy guided her through the crawl space. Gary was next and I followed. Dirt began to rain down on me as Jimmy passed my backpack through the opening. Before I knew what was happening, more rocks were falling. Zippy jostled me aside and reached back for Jimmy.

"Okay, Jimmy! Time to go."

Jimmy was frozen.

"I'm never going to fit through that hole, and you know it," he said in a choked voice.

"Yes you can. Come on!" Zippy said as dust fell into his eyes. "Right now, Jimmy. Move it!"

"Look at me!" Jimmy yelled back. "I'm too fat."

Nobody wanted to admit it, but Jimmy was right. His belly would never pass through the small opening. Thinking fast as the dirt continued to fall, Zippy carefully removed a few more rocks to make the hole larger. But more debris began to rain down. At this rate, the ceiling was sure to collapse again, trapping Jimmy on the other side all by himself.

"Come on, Jimmy. You can do it," I said from the safety of the other side.

"And die in the process?" Jimmy said. "I'm too fat!"

"Well, you better start thinking thin and get your butt moving," Zippy shouted as another cloud of dust rained down. "Move it, Jimmy!"

Jimmy climbed to the top of the debris pile. We watched him poke his face through, but he was right. He was too big for the crawl space Zippy had created.

"I'm stuck," he said, panicking.

"Pull!" Zippy said, looking back at us.

Gary and I reached up, grabbed Zippy's shoulders and pulled with all our might. Jimmy inched forward a bit, but that was it.

"You're going to pull my arms out of their sockets!" he yelled.

"I'm not leaving here without you!" Zippy said. "On three, I want you to exhale all the air you can, and we'll pull you through."

"It's not going to work," Jimmy whimpered.

"Stop whining and focus! You can do this! Can you get any leverage with your feet?"

"I can't," Jimmy said. "I'm kicking but there's nothing to push off of. Wait! Okay … I got something."

"Now exhale," Zippy ordered.

"What?"

"Exhale, Jimmy! Do it now!"

Like the cork of a champagne bottle our dad would pop to the kitchen ceiling on New Year's Eve, Jimmy shot through the hole and landed on top of us. Not a moment later, the entire ceiling started to collapse again.

"Run!" Zippy yelled, as he pulled Jimmy to his feet.

All at once, we sprinted towards the entrance of the cave. Looking back, I heard a sound like thunder and watched the cave collapse behind Zippy like the jaws of a lion. I bolted faster than ever before. A moment later, I could hear the rumble of the waterfall. Safety was near.

Stepping out of the mouth of the cave, I beheld a beautiful sight. The mist of the falls moistened my face, and I knew we were going to be okay. Zippy exited the cave just in time. An instant later, the cave collapsed behind him. He whizzed past me like a speeding bullet, unable to stop his momentum. When he tried, his feet slipped on the wet rocks and he went flying through the roaring waterfall to the other side as if he was on a Slip 'n Slide.

The rest of us ran through the giant sheet of water, only to discover that Zippy had been swallowed up and carried away by the rushing water before us!

Jimmy ran down the trail that was next to the river's edge. "Over there!" he yelled.

Zippy's backpack sprung up in the white water like a fishing bobber. Zippy was being washed downstream. We ran as fast as we could to catch up, but it was no use. The white water was too powerful. Zippy was disappearing downriver before our eyes, but we kept running.

Rounding a bend, we found Jimmy bent over with his head down and his hands on his knees. Out of breath and defeated, we stood in silence as our eyes scanned downriver. There was no sign of Zippy. There was no sign of his backpack. Zippy was gone.

The reality of the situation began to sink in. Nobody knew what to say or do. I felt more alone than I had ever felt before. Nothing in life can ever prepare you for losing a friend. Not like that. The powerless feeling of watching someone get swept away by an angry river was crippling. I did not want to face it. Nobody did. But it was real. This was actually happening, and Zippy was gone.

Snapping out of his stunned gaze, Jimmy started down the trail again.

"Where are you going?" Gary asked, but Jimmy did not answer.

"Jimmy!" Gary said louder this time.

"As long as there's a trail to follow, I'm going this way."

"Jimmy, there's no way he could survive that water. It's freezing," Gary said, walking towards him. "We have to go back the way we came."

"And how are we going to do that?" Jimmy said, turning in the middle of the trail. "The bridge is out. Remember?"

"He's got a point." I said, agreeing with Jimmy.

Gary only looked at me as if to say, "you're not helping the situation."

"Besides, Zippy's going to need our help getting out of here," Jimmy said as he continued to make his way down the trail, mumbling to himself. It was as if he was trying to convince himself that Zippy was going to be okay. But I knew Zippy was gone.

"Jimmy! Stop!"

"Come on you guys, you know Zippy. He's probably sitting on a rock somewhere, waiting for us to catch up," Jimmy said nervously. "It's a good thing I brought my jacket, right? He's going to be cold."

"Jimmy!" Gary said, grabbing his arm.

"Let go of me!" Jimmy replied, not making eye contact with Gary, or anyone for that matter. "Please. Just let me go, okay? I just … I just … I gotta find him."

"Jimmy."

"No."

"Jimmy, he's gone," I said softly, arriving behind Gary.

"No. He's not gone!" Jimmy spun around to face me like a warrior preparing to do battle. "Just shut up, Scooter!"

"Knock it off, Jimmy!" Gary yelled over him, which snapped Jimmy straight. When he finally looked up, he had tears in his eyes. Jaq wrapped her arms around him, but this only made him cry more. Then I realized that I was crying too. Tears of pain ran down my face, carrying memories of Zippy and all the fun times we had shared. It was hard to face.

"If we're going to follow the river back into town," Gary said softly, "we'd better get moving."

When life deals you something this hard, something that cuts deep into the place where friendships and fond memories dwell, your mind struggles to find an answer to the question: Why did this happen? You replay the situation in your mind so many times that the lines begin to blur between what actually happened and what you wish would have happened. In the end, I knew I had to face reality. I would have to accept life without my friend, Zippy.

Then I began to think about Zippy's mom. Somebody would have to tell her. She'd lost her husband only six months earlier, and now this? She would be devastated, and this realization made the situation even worse, if that was possible. The empty feeling inside of me seemed to expand. The hurt sunk even deeper. I had lost a great friend. It all seemed like a bad dream. Zippy was dead, and this was going to change everything. Our lives would never be the same.

TREASURE TIP

If you THINK you can't, you won't.
If you KNOW you can, you will.

27

THE LONG AND
WINDING ROAD HOME

As we followed the river to the sea, the awe and wonderment that had accompanied our trek to Goldstream Falls turned into a foggy memory. Everything was different. The air was different. The way my feet met the ground was different. Even the birds flying overhead were different, somehow. The truth was, we were different and there was no sign of Zippy.

No matter how many times I hit the rewind button in my mind, the outcome was the same. Zippy was gone. I knew it would be impossible to erase the memory, but the more I thought about the brutal truth of my friend dying, the more I realized this was not a memory at all. Losing a friend was a nightmare fully realized.

It took us about an hour to reach the mouth of the river as it emptied into the massive body of the Puget Sound. This was where the cutthroat trout, a freshwater river fish, magically transformed into the saltwater steelhead salmon. The process was truly one of Mother Nature's wonders, but as I thought about it now, I realized that we were transformed, as well. Nothing would ever be the same. Every time I stepped into our fort, I would think of Zippy. Every time we played a game of baseball, I would think of Zippy. Every time I created something out of nothing, I would think of Zippy. I knew if I did not come to grips with this somehow, losing Zippy would haunt me forever.

As we made our way through the shop-lined streets of downtown Woodbury Island, I saw people staring at us. Then, as I looked at the others, I could see why. The adventure had left us covered in dirt, and our faces wore the turmoil of the last five hours of our lives.

It was now around 1:30 p.m., and the inner harbor of Woodbury Island was crawling with people eating lunch, sightseeing, shopping at the vendor carts and relaxing on the benches that dotted the park.

"This way," Gary said, leading us past the majestic Bradford Hotel on the east side of town.

"What do you mean, this way?" Jimmy said, stopping in his tracks. "Where do you think you're going?"

"Home."

"Really? Just like that?"

"What do you want me to do, Jimmy?" Gary replied.

"We have to go to the police and report what happened," Jimmy said, staring Gary down—something he had never done before.

"I don't believe it," Jaq said, gazing across the crowded square.

"What's not to believe?" Gary asked, growing impatient with the futile debate. "We all watched him drown. We walked the entire river and found nothing. Now let's go."

"No. Over there. Look," Jaq replied.

Following the line of her arm, stretched out towards the crowd of people frolicking in the warm afternoon sun, it was hard to tell what she was pointing at.

"Look at what?" Jimmy asked, not sure what to focus on.

"Can't you see? Over there," Jaq said, flicking her hand as if the motion might help focus our attention. "On the park bench! There, over by the ferry docks."

A crowd of tourists blocked my view. But when a young mother pushed her baby's stroller away, I saw Old Man Sheesley sitting on a park bench, hunched over with his hands on his knees.

What is he doing there? I wondered. *Why had he not raced home to uncover the lost treasure? What's he waiting for? Is he gloating? Savoring his victory?*

Before I could answer any of these questions running through my mind, I felt the blood rush to my face with anger. It grabbed hold of me like a huge tidal wave, consuming me without hesitation or permission. I knew our parents did not agree with the saying, "an eye for an eye ...," but the emotion that surged inside of me was undeniable. It was also comforting, somehow. I wanted vengeance. I wanted to blame this old man for the loss of my friend.

I knew what was happening to me. It had been happening during the entire walk downriver. I was mad about losing Zippy, but it was more than that. I was mad about everything. Mad about being shorter than everyone else. Mad for having struck out on the baseball field. Mad about being called the younger brother. Mad because the most popular girl in school would not give me the time of day. Mad at the weather when it rained. Yes, and mad about losing one of my best friends. I was mad, mad, mad!

The funny thing about moments like this, moments when you wish something had never happened, is that they become the moments you never forget. They are the moments that shape who you are. I once heard someone say that there are no mistakes in life—there are only choices. Everything that happens in life is there to guide us towards the next thing, the next lesson, the next opportunity to grow up. Essentially, life is one long process of growing up. No matter how old you are or how old you get, life is about growing up, so you might as well get to growing up while the growing up is good.

Losing Zippy made me take a long, hard look at how I was spending my time. Not the time playing with my friends and going to school, because all that was great—even when it wasn't, if you know what I mean. I was thinking about the time I spent alone with my thoughts. You know, the kind of thoughts that you never share with anyone—like wondering about your place in the world, frustrated that you don't fit in with the crowd or confused about your future. You know, the kind of thoughts that swirl around in your mind so fast that it's hard to see clearly. In reality, all you end up doing is worrying about worrying.

Looking back, I realized that I had spent so much time fantasizing about situations in which my happiness would be a result of something, like hitting a home run or Brandy noticing me. Was this the way I wanted to live my life— with my happiness based on a condition of something happening, and not based on who I was?

I knew the chips were going to fall where they would fall, regardless of how much I worried or how angry I got, so I decided to look at my life from a place of happiness. And that's why, at that moment, I made a decision not to mourn Zippy's death, but to celebrate his life by celebrating mine. I would have fun, meet people and try new things, even if I was afraid. I would resist anger, and wherever I went, whatever I did, I knew Zippy would be with me. At that moment, I became fearless about becoming more of me. Not the me I think other people wanted me to be. Just the me I know I can be—the me I really am!

Gary finally broke my trance by repeating what Jaq had said when she first saw Old Man Sheesley sitting on the bench across the park.

"I don't believe it."

Just as I was about to steer everyone away from thoughts of revenge, I heard a voice behind me—like a spooky voice in a haunted mansion that echoed with never-ending horror.

TREASURE TIP

Every moment in life is a choice.
You get to choose how you're going to react
to any given situation. Choose wisely.

28

RETURNING

"Oh, yes! You can believe it, buddy boy," whispered a ghostly voice.

I froze, not so much from hearing the words themselves or their eerie tone, but because I recognized the voice. If you had told me a moment earlier it was true, I never would have believed it. My eyes blinked to register the swirling vortex of reality I suddenly found myself in. I turned my head nervously towards the voice. Poking his head between Gary and Jimmy like a turtle coming out of its shell was Zippy.

"Believe it like the day is hot, boys, because that is Old Man Sheesley sitting there on that park bench. And inside that coat pocket of his? That's right! Our complete map of Jean Lafitte's lost treasure!"

Was a ghost standing before me? Was a daydream playing tricks on me? I had watched Zippy's backpack disappear in the white water, so I knew this had to be wishful thinking.

"Zippy!" Jaq screamed, leaping into his arms as if it was his birthday.

"Whoa! Easy Jaq," he said, laughing as his knees buckled from the added weight of love. "You're gonna choke me."

"I oughtta knock your block off!" Jimmy said, pushing him from behind. "Come walkin' up on us like it's no big deal."

"Man, we thought you were dead!" I added, colossally happy to see him alive.

"Sorry to disappoint you, Scooter Boy, but I got a lot to do with this life of mine, and dying in some river isn't one of them."

"Good to see ya, Zip," Gary said, slipping his hand into Zippy's for a quick shake of friendship. "You're still kinda wet, though."

"Not as wet as I was a few hours ago," Zippy replied with a laugh. "Anybody cry when they thought I was a goner?"

"I think Jimmy dropped a few tears," Gary said, chuckling.

"Oh, you think this is funny?" Jimmy fired back.

"Yeah? He cried?" Zippy joked back to Gary.

"I'm serious, man," Jimmy continued. "We thought you were dead!"

"All right, calm down. I'm standing right here, you don't have to yell," Zippy said, before turning to Gary. "You'd think ol' Jimmy here's the one who had his life flash before his eyes."

"Is that what happened?" Jaq quickly asked. "Was it like watching a movie of your life? Images scrambling by like a fast-forwarding dream?"

"Jaq, I was swallowing so much water, I'm not sure what I saw, but I will say this: don't let anyone ever call you a sissy for carrying your backpack." Zippy turned to show her his wet backpack, still strapped to his shoulders. "This thing saved my life."

"What do you mean?"

"My backpack was like a life jacket keeping me from going under all that white water rushin' about. Plus, I wasn't about to lose out to a nut-job like Old Man Sheesley."

"So how'd you find your way back?"

"Well, I knew if you rookies didn't die without me blazing the trail for ya, you'd make your way back to the ferry sooner or later. I started to head to the docks when I saw Old Man Sheesley bump into a man, spin around and nearly bump into me before he just kept on walking. It was like he was in a trance or something. The old fart's been sitting on that bench for the past forty-five minutes."

We started to pepper him with questions.

"Does he have the map?"

"Did he put the four pieces together?"

"Does it lead to the lost treasure?"

"Would you let him talk already?" Gary said, reeling us in.

"Yes, he has the map. And yes, he put the four pieces together, but the crazy old geezer's just been sittin' there talkin' to himself ever since. Every few minutes, he takes out the map, looks it over with that crinkled frown of his, places it back into the cylinder, then slips it into his right jacket pocket. See? Watch. There he goes again."

Our eyes moved to the park bench and Old Man Sheesley mirrored Zippy's description right down to the crinkled frown on his line-creased forehead.

"He can't figure it out," I said quickly.

"We gotta get our hands on that map," Gary said even quicker.

"Let's jump him!" Jimmy suggested.

"Okay, Hercules! We'll jump him," Gary said, shooting Jimmy's suggestion down.

"Brains before brawn, you guys," Zippy declared. "Brains before brawn."

"Brains before brawn? What are you talking about? Let's jump him, I'm tellin' you. We outnumber the guy five to one," Jimmy rallied. "And he's like a million years old."

"*And* he's got a gun. Duh!" Gary snapped a glance at Jimmy to remind him of how insanely stupid the idea of jumping the old man was.

"Fine, then let's report him to the cops."

"And say what, smarty pants?" Zippy snapped. "Gee, Officer, that old man stole our treasure map ... *Yeah? Where you from? ...* Port Townsend, sir.... *Yeah? Whatcha doing over here on Woodbury Island? ...* Looking for buried treasure ... *Yeah? Well, then that treasure is going to belong to the people of Woodbury Island ...* Bzzzzzzz! Wrong answer. Care to play again?"

"Good to have you back, Zip," Gary said, smiling at Zippy's quick, cut-down wit.

"Back and better than ever, baby. Not to worry, Jimmy. I worked out a plan that's gonna get us the map." Zippy continued to stare at Old Man Sheesley while he talked. "Scooter Boy? You got any of your mom's saltwater taffy in that backpack of yours?"

"I think I got a few pieces left. Why?"

"Because we're gonna need 'em."

"For what?"

"For the bomb."

"The bomb?"

"What bomb?"

"You're back? Better than ever?" Jimmy quipped. "I've heard some duds before, but a saltwater taffy bomb? Don't make me laugh."

Zippy stared at Jimmy until Jimmy felt uncomfortable.

"What? You know it sounds like a stupid idea!"

"No, Jimmy. You want to know what's really stupid?

"Oh, right, this is where you tell me what's wrong with me again."

"I don't need to," Zippy said with an expression on his face that could only be described as one that bordered on sympathy.

"Oh yeah?" Jimmy said, nodding his head like one of those bobble-headed dogs in the back window of a car. "Gee, Zippy, why's that?"

"No matter what we do or where we go, you're the first one to discover what's wrong with the situation or why we shouldn't do something. And do you want to know why?"

"I wanna know why!" Jaq added, which was kind of funny.

"Say what you will about Old Man Sheesley and that crazy letter of his, but if you were listening close enough, some of it made pretty good sense."

"What are you talkin' about?" Jimmy scoffed at Zippy's revelation.

"Jimmy, you're so frustrated and busy trying *not* to be your big brother that you're missing out on what it's like to be you. How do you know you can't make a bomb with saltwater taffy until you try?" Zippy did not wait for an answer. "You think Ben Franklin went kite flying in the rain because he didn't believe there was something more to discover?"

Zippy softened his approach and stepped towards Jimmy, who had become sullen and was on the verge of tears. "Jimmy, all I'm saying is when you look for something wrong, you cut yourself off from possibility and the moment of discovery. It's the secret of every great inventor. You gotta remain open to any possibility that might present itself."

Even though he was talking to Jimmy, the words hit me like a like a pallet of cinder blocks falling off the back of a dump truck.

"Wow, man! I just had this same conversation with myself right after you died ... well, when I thought you died ... but you didn't die ... but when I thought you did, it made me think about a lot of things, and—"

"Me too," Jaq said, joining in.

"Well, great. Zip, if you don't mind dyin' once a week, I'm sure you can get us all through high school," Gary said, half joking. "We can talk about all that warm and fuzzy stuff later. Right now, let's focus on getting our map back."

"Yeah. The game starts in three hours, if anyone still cares about that," I added, looking at my watch.

"No, not unless we're cool," Zippy said, turning back to Jimmy. "Come on, man. Are we cool?"

Jimmy did not want it to be cool. He was embarrassed, and Zippy knew that, so he stepped in closer. "I don't mean to call you out in front of everybody, but if we're going to be friends, the kind of friends we all talk about being, we have to be able to tell it like it is. Right? The good. The bad. The ugly. The whole thing, kind of like you did with me on the bridge this morning. And hey, this might sound weird, but I was proud of you for knocking me on my butt, too."

"Really?" Jimmy asked, pushing back the tears that had formed in the corners of his eyes.

"Yeah, I deserved it. You know, my dad always said, 'Son, you must stand up for who you are. If you don't, someone else will tell you what to do, and you'll regret it for the rest of your life.' Now, you ready to make a saltwater taffy bomb or what?"

Jimmy did not answer, but he managed to find a smile somewhere.

"Okay, good," Zippy continued, pivoting around to face us again. "Jaq, you go over to that candy store and get us a pack of Mentos, mint flavored. Scooter Boy, you find us some rope. We need a good twenty feet if you can find it. Gary, I need you to find us a wad of fishing line. And Jimmy, I need you to find me a soda. You know, one of those new plastic bottles we had at Fatman's last week."

"Wait, what's the soda for?" Jimmy asked.

"What?"

"The soda, what's it for?"

"Oh, nothing. I'm just super thirsty," Zippy replied.

Jimmy's eyes grew wide as if he was being fooled with again, but Zippy relented.

"Easy tiger, I'm just messin' with ya. The plastic soda bottle is the most important part of the bomb, and I need *you* to get it."

"But how's a bottle of soda going to be part of—" Jimmy stopped his inquiry short, remembering what Zippy had said. "Guess we're going to find out, right?"

"Now you're cookin' with gas, baby. Cookin' with gas for sure," Zippy said, smiling. "We'll meet by the giant Slurpee machine cart in five minutes."

"You mean right next to the two cops on horseback?" I asked.

"That's right, Scooter. Right next to the two cops on horseback."

We scattered, each with our own task in mind. I could not stop the smile from creeping across my face, because this moment felt like old times again. It was good to have Zippy back, and while the whole thing had been a roller coaster ride of emotions, I was not going to forget the agreement I had made with myself. Never again would I let anger run my life. Those two hours I spent thinking Zippy was dead had changed my life forever.

TREASURE TIP

Anger preoccupies the mind and
cuts you off from an inspired thought.

29

THE HUNT

Have you ever noticed how difficult it is to find something when the clock is ticking? It's as if the something you're looking for is hiding from you on purpose. But isn't that the way it is with most things in life? When you are not looking, you find it, but when you are looking, it's nowhere to be found. It's like cramming for a test or doing homework at the last minute. The ticking clock just seems to make the process harder.

So there I was in downtown Woodbury Island, looking for twenty feet of rope. Why couldn't I be the one to get a coke bottle? Or maybe even the pack of Mentos? Of course, I had to find the hard item, but that was always the case. Then I realized I was looking at the task as a burden and not an honor. Zippy had given me the hard item because he knew I could find it. He had faith in me, so why was I not having faith in myself?

With that, I simply changed my mind and embraced my new thought of confidence with open arms. My pace quickened. I was determined to find the rope, even if it killed me. Filled with anticipation, I passed my pocketknife from one hand to the other. My head felt as if it was on a swivel, scanning my surroundings for any sign of rope. As my mind drifted to the pangs of hunger growling in my belly, I saw something out of the corner of my eye.

Stopping short, I backpedaled to the entrance of an alley that ran behind a row of shops. There was a knick-knack shop and a shoe repair shop, and at the end of the alley, I saw a beautiful woman dressed in a white chef's coat exiting through a bakery's back screen door. She was probably in her late twenties, and it was like I was watching a commercial for laundry soap the way the sunlight washed over her. She was placing wet aprons on a long clothesline made of rope.

While my task was to find a piece of rope, I found myself lost in watching the lady hang the aprons on the clothesline. She looked like Miss America. Then I realized she was a grown-up version of Brandy Larson with her blonde hair dancing in the wind. One apron—beautiful. Two aprons—stunning. Three aprons ... four. When she reached back for the fifth apron in the clothes hamper, her eyes found me watching her from the end of the alley. Her smile almost knocked me over. Flustered by her beauty, I ducked out of sight behind the old brick walls of the knickknack shop.

Catching my breath, I peered around the corner to see the beautiful woman—this muffin maker, this perfect example of beauty—finishing her work. Satisfied, she straightened her chef's coat and disappeared into the bakery again. As the screen door shut, I snapped out of the imaginary soap commercial running through my mind and was on the move again.

I flicked open my pocketknife and slashed one end of the clothesline. Out of respect for "Miss America," I took the aprons in my arms and dumped them back into the whicker hamper. I coiled the rope and cut the other end. Just as I snapped shut the blade of my pocketknife, I heard the screen door spring open again.

Now, being thirteen years old, I run pretty much on instinct when faced with trouble. For the most part, the old adage of fight or flight turned out to be flight for me. I was never one for the fight unless my life depended on it. I knew I could run like a jackrabbit, but today I was done running. Maybe it was the emotional stress that came from thinking I had lost a best friend, or maybe it was the conversations I'd had with myself about life during the long hike down from the cave, but at that moment, I was done running. I guess you could say I was at the end of my rope.

"What are you doing with my clothesline?" she asked in a voice that sounded different than what I had expected. I had imagined Snow White, or maybe the lady from *The Sound of Music*, but not the gruff inquiry I heard. I took a deep breath and slowly turned to face her.

The corners of her mouth were drawn tight and her eyes were narrow. She was like a tiger ready to pounce, but man, was she ever pretty.

"Are you just going to stand there?" she asked. "Don't you talk?"

"Well, ma'am, I live in Port Townsend, and this morning, at about 3:45 a.m., me and my friends—"

"My friends and I," she said, correcting me.

"Yes ma'am, my friends and I, well, we were—"

I stalled when I looked into her beautiful blue eyes. There I was, about to get in trouble, and all I could do was think about how pretty her eyes were. It was as if her beauty had hypnotized me the way a snake charmer charmed a snake.

"Go on, then. Out with it!" she ordered.

"Yes, ma'am. At 3:45 this morning, we were stowaways on a cargo ship. We came over here and almost got eaten by a black bear, which was shot by two hunters who were hunting illegally. Then we were double-crossed by an old man I thought I could trust, who tried to kill us by making the cave collapse. I watched a friend die—only he didn't die! He lived because his backpack kept him afloat, and now that old man who double-crossed us has all the pieces to the map for the lost treasure of Jean Lafitte in his pocket and we need twenty feet of rope for some kind of saltwater taffy bomb our friend is going to make."

It was like I suddenly woke up from a dose of truth serum. I do not think I had ever been so truthful in all my life. It actually felt good, so I continued.

"Truth is, ma'am, I don't really know what the rope is for, but I was supposed to find a rope, and yours is the only one I could find, and now I have two minutes to meet everyone or the old man's going to get away with our map, and we'll never find the treasure, plus I have a really big baseball game today before the fireworks show, and I'm hoping to sit with the girl I have a crush on."

The muffin-maker just stared at me.

"Been kind of a long day." I added this like a cherry on top of a sundae of truth.

With a quizzical look, she looked me over, tilted her head to one side and smiled. "That's quite a story."

"Yes ma'am."

"Then I guess you'd best be on your way now."

"Yes, ma'am, I guess so," I said as I walked past her, exiting the alley before turning back to thank her. She just smiled and carried the hamper full of aprons back inside the bakery.

Maybe she had children, I thought as I searched for a reason why she let me go just now. Maybe she wanted children. Maybe she had taken pity on me. I did not know. Sure, I could have run from her, but sometimes the truth is the best option, and maybe that was why she let me go, however unbelievable my story might have sounded. I'm not saying I told the truth all the time, but I knew that when I did, I felt a lot better inside.

I was the last to arrive under the giant maple tree, which provided a shady canopy over an elaborate Slurpee machine cart. This Slurpee machine was a brilliant concoction. It was part Slurpee machine and part amusement park, because of how the clear tubing circled high in the air, shuttling the sugary liquid through the cooling coils in the base of the machine. It worked too, because there was a line of kids oohing and aahing at the machine's carnival-like artistry.

Zippy was like the commander of a squad of soldiers, the way he was using hand signals to communicate. Seeing this, Gary grabbed the rope from my hands, moved up behind the park bench where Old Man Sheesley sat and tied one end of the rope around the leg of the wooden bench. He carefully fed the rope out and returned.

Meanwhile, Zippy was instructing me to follow his lead as he unwrapped a few pieces of Mom's saltwater taffy.

Popping the candy into his mouth, he worked it into the shape of a Tootsie Roll. He unscrewed the cap of the plastic soda bottle and poured out half of the soda before sliding the sticky saltwater taffy mess into the bottle. It was hard to chew a piece of Mom's saltwater taffy and not swallow it, especially when the piece inside of my mouth was Mom's specialty — root beer float.

With the saltwater taffy Tootsie Rolls now inside the bottle, Zippy motioned to Jaq to open the pack of Mentos she'd got from the candy store on the corner. One by one, she handed the sugarcoated candies to Zippy, which he pressed onto a large nail he had scavenged from a nearby construction site. He was like a bartender skewering olives. I had no idea of what he was building, but he sure looked like he knew what he was doing, so I did not question him. Nobody did.

Placing the flat head of the nail inside the plastic cap of the soda bottle, Zippy put out his hand to Jimmy the way a surgeon reaches out to a nurse for a scalpel. Jimmy handed him a magnet; Zippy had torn it out of a transistor radio speaker that he had blown up with one of his homemade M-80s a week ago. We all watched as Zippy placed the magnet on top of the plastic cap, and it drew the head of the nail to the inside of the cap. He turned to Jaq one last time, and she handed him a looped piece of fishing line that Gary had found. Zippy took the end, tied it around the magnet and put the skewered Mentos inside of the soda bottle. Carefully, he screwed the cap back onto the plastic soda bottle and shot us a smile.

With the completed saltwater taffy bomb in his clutches, Zippy moved through the crowd to a point behind the park bench where Old Man Sheesley sat. He carefully set the soda bottle down, fed out the fishing line and returned like an army man drawing out a long fuse of an explosive charge.

"Okay, Gary. You know what to do."

"Wait! Hold on. What's going on? Someone, fill me in," I said.

"Last to show, last to know," Jimmy reminded me.

Touché, Jimmy!

Gary was on the move with the other end of the rope. I had no idea what I was a party to, so all I could do was watch and wait. The anticipation consumed me. What happened next, however, I never could have imagined. It was the most amazing thing I had ever seen.

TREASURE TIP

The truth will always set you free.

30

A STICKY SITUATION

SAWEEET!

I think every kid dreams about being James Bond at one point or another, and watching my friends execute Zippy's plan was one of those moments for me.

From the safety behind the giant maple tree, I watched Gary carefully weave the rope tied to the park bench through the wheel of the massive Slurpee cart, and then over to the two horses that belonged to the policemen. He paused as they glanced his way while sipping coffee from a nearby coffee vendor cart. Acting like he was simply admiring their horses, Gary fastened the end of the rope to the saddle of one of the horses. He returned to our position and gave Zippy the thumbs up.

When I looked to Zippy to find out what the thumbs up meant, Zippy turned his attention to Old Man Sheesley as he prepared for his map-studying routine. Zippy gave Jimmy the thumbs up. Without hesitation, Jimmy grabbed some BBs from Zippy's backpack and popped one into his mouth. Raising a drinking straw to his lips, Jimmy aimed his BB-spit-wad at the horses. The look on my face said it all: *He's going to do what?*

Jimmy puffed his cheeks like a puffer fish and shot the BB spit-wad with all his might, but the BB was too heavy. The shot barely went five feet. Zippy's head snapped towards Old Man Sheesley, who was finishing his map routine. This time, however, it looked as though he was preparing to leave.

Thinking fast, Zippy grabbed the straw, popped a BB into his own mouth and gave it a try—but it was no use! The BBs were just too heavy for a shot from that distance. Zippy grabbed a handful of BBs and gave them to Jaq.

"Jaq, you're up!" he said. "Pin the tail on the donkey."

Jaq was fearless. She took the handful of BBs and fired them at the horses as if she was turning a double play. When the BB's hit the bulbous rumps of the horses, they reacted like a riding jockey had just slapped them with a riding crop at the Kentucky Derby. Rearing up on their hind legs, the two horses bolted forward. When their front legs finally lowered to the pavement, they took off.

The cops ditched their coffee cups and scrambled to grab the reins of their horses, but it was too late. The rope tied to the saddle snapped taut and flipped the Slurpee machine high in the air the way a house cat flips a captured mouse. People scattered as the Slurpee machine did a full cartwheel in the air before crashing to the pavement. Frozen sugar water from the elaborate tubing shot up like Old Faithful, the geyser in Yellowstone National Park.

The park bench whipped out from under Old Man Sheesley's butt and shot sparks across the concrete as it raced after the spooked horses, drawing the attention of the crowd with them. Flat on his back, Old Man Sheesley sat up and returned his gaze to his own predicament. Seeing this, Zippy yanked on the fishing line connected to the magnet, which snapped off the cap, causing the nail-skewered Mentos to sink to the bottom of the plastic soda bottle.

Old Man Sheesley, sitting up from his fall, paused when he noticed the curious soda bottle hissing at him a few feet away. His eyes squinted, looking more closely as the soda began to foam from the chemical reaction between the mint-flavored Mentos candy and the carbonated soda. His gaze slowly rose and fell upon the group of us gathered together under the maple tree in anticipation. His eyes narrowed further with anger. When he realized that we were covering our ears, the old man's eyes widened. Just as he scrambled to his feet, the saltwater taffy bomb exploded.

KABLOOEY!

Gobs of saltwater taffy plastered his aging face, knocking him backward and to the ground. His grubby hands pawed at his face, trying to clear the sticky goo from his beard and eyelashes. Even though Zippy said he would retrieve the map himself, Jimmy shot forward like a football player running for the goal line. Skidding to a stop at Old Man Sheesley's side, Jimmy reached into Old Man Sheesley's coat and grabbed the cylinder.

"I got it!" he said, turning towards us in celebration.

"Not so fast, Porky!" Old Man Sheesley said, grabbing Jimmy's ankle. Already halfway there, Zippy accelerated his run, plowed into Old Man Sheesley and knocked him over.

POW! CRASH! BOOM!

Old Man Sheesley fell backwards and to the ground, coughing the air back into his lungs.

"Time to go, Jimmy," Zippy said, grabbing Jimmy's arm.

Seeing this, we all broke for the ferry the way we'd run to the schoolyard when the recess bell rang at school. Jaq and I smiled at each other and bolted up the massive gangway to board the ferry. As my pace quickened, Zippy grabbed my arm to a stop.

"Wait!"

"But the ferry," I said, watching the others continue ahead. "The gates are closing."

"Hold on. Wait for it," he said with his mischievous smile, looking back towards Old Man Sheesley.

As the cops returned to the scene to survey the chaos, Old Man Sheesley began to yell, pointing in our direction. One of the cops looked our way, but before his eyes could locate us, there was a second explosion in a trash can across the park, which blew the lid sky high.

KABOOM!

The cops scrambled towards the explosion, and Zippy smiled like a painter admiring his latest canvas. The ferry horn blared its final horn.

"Now we can go," Zippy said, and we started for the gates.

"Was that you? The explosion?"

"Triple-fused M-80, Scooter Boy," he said running ahead of me. "Always good to have a secondary diversion in case things don't go according to the plan."

"Good to know."

We arrived at the ticket gate just in time as Gary handed the ticket person the last of our ferry ticket stash. We had made it. We had the map, and we were on our way home. Victory was ours.

Buzzing with excitement, we scurried up the stairs of the ferry and found a corner booth on the passenger deck. The sun bled though the windows of the cabin, and we breathed a collective sigh of relief. Sitting in the warm sunlight was quite a departure from the cold deck of the cargo ship on our ride over this morning—which, when I thought about it, seemed like a very long time ago. Come to think of it, the past two days were a blur, but worth every second.

"Okay, Jimmy. Let's get a look at this puppy and find our treasure," Zippy said, smiling wide.

"Oh yes! The map," Jimmy said.

Digging into his coat pocket, his smile suddenly dropped. Urgently, he felt his back pockets ... then his front pockets. He was like a police officer patting down a robbery suspect for weapons. Panic quickly replaced his blank stare.

"Stop messing around." Gary leaned forward.

"Seriously, I'm not. I put it right here in my pocket," Jimmy said with his voice trailing off into his own isolation of panic. My heart sank into my stomach like a cannonball. We had come all this way to end up empty-handed? How could it be? Had Jimmy dropped the cylinder during the mad dash for the ferry? Surely he would have noticed. Surely one of us would have noticed, but we were running so fast, anything was possible.

"You lost it?" Zippy leaned forward, flabbergasted as the moment unfolded before us. Then, slowly, Jimmy revealed his own mischievous smile. He'd got us back for all the times we'd got him. He'd fooled us, and fooled us good.

"Good one, Jimmy." Gary smiled, patting Jimmy on the shoulders.

"Back and better than ever, baby," Jimmy said, mimicking Zippy as he pulled the cylinder from his jacket pocket.

"All right. I'll give it to you—you got me! Now hand her over," Zippy said cheerfully.

He reached for the cylinder, but Jimmy held onto it until Zippy looked into his eyes. Jimmy smiled one last time before Zippy jerked it away. Yes, Jimmy was proud of his ruse—so much so that he made sure he made eye contact with the rest of us.

Unlike the last time Zippy had opened the cylinder, methodically and with great care, it was like Christmas morning the way he let the cap fly off and bounce across the table like a piece of discarded wrapping paper.

Pulling out the now complete treasure map, Zippy unrolled it and spread it out on the table. We each held a corner of the map to flatten it out. Our smiles were wide and our hearts pounded with anticipation. I think this was the most exciting thing we had ever been through—and we had been through a lot, especially during the last two days. Sure, we had done a lot of hard work to get where we were, but hard work always makes a victory that much sweeter.

"Okay, turn it. I can't see—" Zippy said.

"Yeah, it's kind of hard to make out," Jimmy added.

But turning the map did not do any good. The smiles on our faces faded like the docks of the distant Woodbury Island Harbor. The four quadrants of the map fit together perfectly, but upon closer inspection, the map was missing the all-important X-marks-the-spot. Everybody who was anybody knew that X always marked the spot on a treasure map, but our map did not have one.

"I don't understand," Jaq mused, looking up for help. "The trail doesn't lead anywhere."

"No wonder he was just sittin' there all confused on that park bench," Gary added with a laugh. "His whole life has been about finding that treasure, and now—nothing!"

"What are you laughing at?" Zippy said.

"Because I think it's hilarious," Gary replied. "Tommy's dad was right. The whole thing's a hoax and a huge waste of time."

"It can't be," I said, spinning the map in my direction for another look.

"You think they have hotdogs in the cafeteria?" Jimmy said, sitting back in the booth, searching the passenger cabin for the cafeteria.

Zippy sank back into the cushioned seats as defeat enveloped him.

"Sorry, man," Gary said, putting his arm around him. "I know this—"

"—doesn't make sense," Zippy replied in a low rumble.

"Come on, you guys," I said. "We just started looking at the map. Give it some time."

"And that's probably exactly what Old Man Sheesley said to himself on that park bench," Zippy continued. "He sat there for over forty-five minutes, and he's been treasure hunting all his life."

Tired, weary and defeated, we sat in silence. It was three o'clock, and we had been going non-stop for over twelve hours. It had been a long day and the map before us showed a trail that led in circles. It was useless.

"Sure was a good time, though," Jaq finally said, breaking the silence.

"And hey, I can honestly say I was chased by a black bear and survived," Gary said with a laugh. "Jimmy, you should've seen your face when you went runnin' by me like a wild caveman."

"Not a big fan of bears," Jimmy said, joining the laughter, which slowly died down into silence again.

We were disappointed and there was no hiding it, but Zippy was flat out mad. He grabbed the map, crushed it into a ball and threw it into the trash can against the windows of the cabin. The shot was a perfect swish. It was hard to believe, but the treasure map was now a worthless piece of trash.

"So, Jimmy? You think they have hot dogs in that cafeteria?" Zippy said, conceding defeat.

"Only one way to find out," Jimmy said, exchanging a smile with him.

"Let's eat," Gary said as we climbed out of the booth.

But I could not take the defeat so easily. My mind was on the treasure map resting in the sunlight atop the trash can.

Gary crossed back for me.

"It's junk, Scooter. Let it be."

"Sure would be a cool souvenir from the adventure, though."

"You mean a worthless souvenir. Come on. Let's go get a dog. We gotta get our energy up for the game."

As Gary turned and followed the others, I went over to the trash can. I smiled, hearing the laughter of my friends, and while we were disappointed by the whole situation, it had been one of the best days of our lives. Jimmy and Zippy walked towards the cafeteria like two buddies, which would never have happened had we not gone on this adventure. The things I learned about myself, the things I learned about my anger and how it had stopped my own happiness, were worth it. It was all worth it.

Looking into the trash can, I saw the crumpled map in the sunlight shining through the cabin windows. Looking closer, I saw something I had not seen before. I had not seen it because it had not been there before this moment. Something was happening to the map.

It's because of the sunlight, I thought.

The windows were like a magnifying glass. Peering down, I saw a series of lines forming on the old parchment paper.

I reached my hand into the trash can and grabbed the map. Quickly unfolding it so the sunlight could wash over the entire surface, I watched brown lines spider across the parchment. No wonder we could not make sense of the thing! The real map had been drawn with invisible ink, which was now being activated by the magnified sunlight coming through the window panes. I could not believe it. I was now holding a complete map that showed the way to the lost treasure of Jean Lafitte.

TREASURE TIP

You have to be willing to go the extra mile.

31

THE COOTIES

As I watched the lines spider across the rest of the parchment paper, I looked up to find a very large lumberjack-type of man staring at me. He must have been six and a half feet tall, if not seven. His feet were cradled in large work boots and his jeans were worn and frayed. This was a tough man. He was a man's man, and he was looking right at me.

Turning away from him, I blocked the trash can with my body and acted as if nothing was out of the ordinary. Quickly folding the map, I stuffed it into the front pocket of my jeans, and found myself walking away from the prying eyes of the lumberjack behind me.

I turned left into a hallway and followed the signs to the bathroom. Rounding the corner, I stole a quick glance over my shoulder to discover that the lumberjack was following me. His giant strides were right behind me now. My heart was racing, and his pace was quickening. What did he want? Who was he, and why was he following me?

Thinking fast, I flanked to the right and stopped in front of a crowded booth of people.

Safety in numbers, I thought.

But the lumberjack walked even closer. I slowly turned to discover that his massive boots had stopped right behind me. Waiting for his giant lumberjack hand to grab my neck, I turned to face him. As my eyes moved slowly upwards, I realized that he was not looking at me. He was looking past me. Turning around to follow his gaze, I saw a girl about seven years old running towards him.

"Daddy!" she cried with excitement.

He scooped her up and cradled her in his giant arms. The lumberjack's wife arrived a moment later. She smiled at the love before her, and it was at that moment that I realized my imagination was working overtime. This treasure hunt had made my perception of things, people and just about everything, skeptical and exaggerated. I guess you can talk yourself into or out of anything if you think about it long enough.

With my heartbeat returning to normal, I ducked into the bathroom and entered one of the empty stalls. Flipping down the toilet seat, I sat down and pulled out the map. As I did so, I made a great discovery. In my haste to hide the map from the lumberjack, I had perfectly folded over one of its corners. The brown lines created by the magnified sunlight perfectly met the lines on the treasure map's circular trail. I folded the next corner, and it too lined up with the brown lines revealed by the sun. I folded the two remaining corners and lined them up at the center. Could the mystery be this simple?

With the corners now folded into the center, I creased each fold carefully so as not to damage the delicate parchment. With all the corners folded, I could not believe what I was looking at. The treasure map had taken the form of a cootie catcher. Made through a process known as origami, which is the Japanese art of paper folding, a cootie catcher was a fortune telling game dating back centuries.

When I opened the jaws of the cootie catcher, I could see how the brown spider lines mixed with the map's drawings to form an X-marks-the-spot across the four tips of the cootie catcher. When I opened the four flaps, I discovered I was looking at a schematic drawing of the Lafitte Public Library back home. I suddenly felt the engines of the ferryboat shudder and heard the loud horn signal that we were docking in the harbor.

I exited the bathroom, buzzing with more excitement than ever, and heard the laughter of my friends rising over the chatter on the passenger deck as people prepared to disembark. Our booth was alive with the signs of friendship. At that moment, I realized that Old Man Sheesley had been right about one thing: this was what life was about—the friendships and love you shared with others. Having this revelation at thirteen years old was kind of cool. I realized that the friendships we had were stronger than any treasure ever conceived—or discovered, for that matter.

All this made me think of Old Man Sheesley and what his life had turned into because of the treasure hunt. The pursuit of the treasure had consumed him. He was the example, in my opinion, of loneliness brought on by obsession. The obsession had been so strong that he had not been able to find his way back to friendship and love. He was even afraid of talking to Ms. Benson, the object of his desire, and that made me sad. His obsession with finding the treasure had made him so paranoid that he had lived a life of seclusion and loneliness. If the cootie-catcher map led us to the treasure, I wondered how it would affect our lives. I wondered how people would treat us, and more importantly, how we would treat each other, because right now, things were perfect just the way they were.

With this running through my mind, my hand slipped the cootie catcher into the back pocket of my jeans. My discovery could wait. Perhaps I would tell them after the baseball game, but I did not want to miss out on what was happening right now. I did not want to miss out on the opportunity to laugh, not because of some treasure discovery, but in the purity of our friendships.

We ran down the gangplank to the Port Townsend Harbor, dodged our way through the line of cars waiting to board the ferry and jumped onto our bikes. Time was not on our side. We had to race home, change into our uniforms and make it to the ballpark in less than half an hour.

Scattering like a shotgun blast, each of us took our own shortcut home. Gary and I ended up racing down Water Street together, but when I looked across Town Square at the Lafitte Public Library, my feet slowed down on the pedals. Before I knew it, I had rolled to a stop.

"What are you doing?" Gary said, looking over his shoulder as he continued to ride. When I did not answer, he circled back to my location. "What are you doing?" he asked again, power-sliding his bike beside me. "We got to boogie! The game starts in twenty minutes."

"Yeah, I know, but ... I need a favor," I said with a straight face. He nodded, signaling that I should continue. "Grab my uniform and bring it to the dugout?

"Why?"

"Because there's something I need to check out."

"Let it go, Bro. You need to start thinking about the game."

I knew he was right, but I needed to find out if the cootie-catcher map in my pocket was real or just another dead end in a long line of dead ends.

"You know Tommy's going to be gunnin' for you again."

"I'm not worried about Tommy," I said, looking him directly in the eye. "Gary, please. I just ... have to ... check something out."

"All right, but promise me you'll be there."

"Yeah, like I'm going to miss the game," I said with a laugh.

As I turned my bike towards the library, Gary called out after me, "Hey Scott! I had a great time today!"

"Me too, Bro," I said, before I pedaled to the library as fast as I could.

TREASURE TIP

Never, ever, ever give up.

32

ONE LAST TRY

As I pushed open the heavy library doors, my heart quickened with anticipation. The soles of my Wallabees chirped against the marble floor of the grand hallway, as if to announce my arrival.

Pulling the cootie-catcher treasure map from my pocket, I tried to calm myself. With all that we had been through, I did not want my hopes to be dashed by another dead end. The treasure hunt had been a heartbreaking experience, so I wanted to remain as grounded as I could. That was easier said than done, because this treasure hunt was the coolest thing I had ever been through.

Stopping at the crossroads of the grand hallway, I stared at the floor plan display to familiarize myself with my surroundings. Then I followed the map's instructions down a side hallway that I had never taken before.

Moments later, I found myself standing before a door marked, "Authorized Personnel Only." I reached out to test the doorknob. As fate would have it, the door was unlocked. Why would a door marked "Authorized Personnel Only" be unlocked? This was odd, but I did not have time to question why things were happening—not after the past forty-eight hours of my life. I had done things I never would have dreamed of, plus I had to move and move fast.

As I pushed the door open, I heard my name called from behind me. It was Ms. Benson, exiting her office down the hall. She was carrying two round Tupperware containers filled with baked goods. This was not an uncommon occurrence, because Ms. Benson loved to hold bake sales during our baseball games.

"Scott?" she asked, but I could not move. I was frozen stiff like an ice sculpture in the middle of December. "What are you doing here?" she asked, walking towards me.

As I released the door, I had to hide the treasure map quickly, so I slipped it into my pocket. Mission accomplished, but I still had no excuse for my actions.

"Shouldn't you be at the baseball field?" she said, as if ignoring my attempt to enter a room I was not allowed into.

"Yes, ma'am. I … was just going to use the bathroom," I said.

That was a lame excuse. She knew that I knew where the bathrooms were. So much for creativity in the face of fear!

"The bathrooms aren't through that door," she said, looking directly at me now. "You know they're in the main hallway. I'm not sure why this door is open anyway. Nothing's up there but pigeon poop."

"Yes, ma'am," I replied.

"Here, hold these," she said, handing me the boxes of baked goods so she could spin the lock on the back of the doorknob. I knew fate was working on my behalf because the door was open when it was supposed to be locked. But what was I going to do now? My mind wondered but had no immediate answers.

I watched the door slowly swing shut and handed Ms. Benson her Tupperware boxes. As she turned to walk away, I expertly slipped the cootie-catcher map from my back pocket and slid it between the latch of the door and the door jam. I would come back after Ms. Benson left for the ballpark and continue my search, but when I looked up and saw a security guard walking towards us, I began to make quick conversation with Ms. Benson. I needed to call her attention away from the approaching security guard.

"So, another bake sale fundraiser at the ball game, huh?"

"You make sure and tell your teammates to stop by for a cookie. They're two for ten cents," she replied as her eyes settled on the security guard.

"What kind of cookies do you have? Chocolate chip?"

"Yes," she replied quickly, almost as if she was going to address the unlocked door with the security guard, but I quickly interrupted her again.

"What about peanut butter? Do you have peanut butter?" I asked as the security guard brushed past us. "My mom makes the best oatmeal cookies ever," I said in rapid-fire cadence. "Yeah, she uses chocolate chips in 'em and—"

Ms. Benson turned and called out after the security guard. "Charles, sweetie?"

My heart sank. If she told him about the unlocked door,

he would surely double-check it and find the cootie-catcher map sticking in the latch!

"Yes, Ms. Benson?" Charles said, turning around, which was a good thing because he was right in front of the door and had not seen the map. Not yet, anyway. My eyes shifted back and forth between the map, the security guard and Ms. Benson, who still had not spoken. Time was standing still before me.

"You can go ahead and close up early if you'd like. With everyone at the big game, I'm sure it will be slower than molasses in here," Ms. Benson said with a smile. "You're welcome to help out with the bake sale if you'd like."

"Sounds great, ma'am. I'm sure my wife would love to help," he said, walking back towards us. "Would you like me to help you carry those to your car?"

"Why Charles, that would be great," she replied, handing him the Tupperware boxes before turning back to me. "Don't be late to your own game now, Scott. Hurry to that bathroom so Charles can lock up."

"Wouldn't miss it," I said, walking towards the bathrooms in the main hallway. When I finally heard them exit through the front doors, I spun around and bolted for the cootie catcher. Pushing the door open, I grabbed the map and flew up the stairs to the bell tower.

At the top, I opened a second door to a giant fluttering sound that attacked me without warning. The sound knocked me backward and to the ground. Then I realized it was just a bunch of pigeons scattering out through the vents of a dusty space. A bunch of crazy pigeons had nothing on a grunting bear or a raging river, so I popped to my feet without delay.

I was standing before a small, dust-filled room, about six by six feet. The walls were made of wood, and the sunlight bled through the slats of the vents through which the pigeons came and went. Ms. Benson was right—the floor was coated with years, if not decades, of pigeon poop.

Pulling out the cootie catcher, I unfolded the two flaps and stared at the map. A series of markings were just below the X-marks-the-spot. Scanning the room, I saw a poop-covered ladder built into the north wall.

Even though adrenaline was flowing through me faster than a jet airplane, my actions slowed. With each step, my Wallabees sunk into a good five inches of pigeon poop. I had not even reached the ladder and I was already about to gag from the squishy sounds of the floor. It was like walking through a bucket of stinking mud, which suddenly gave me an idea. All I had to do was convince myself, despite the awful smell, that the poop was nothing more than five inches of mud. Sure, it was silly, but I had to think of something because I had to get moving. Game time was drawing closer with every second I wasted.

I opened the hatch-like door at the top of the ladder and pulled myself onto the wooden platform under the massive bell. The vantage point was super cool. It was even cooler than Fatman's roof, and we all knew how cool that was. Turning to my left, I could see Pacheco Park in the distance. As if the clock ticking in my head was not loud enough already, it started to pound as soon as I saw Coach Palmer taking infield with my teammates. I had to get to work!

Comparing the cootie-catcher map to my surroundings, I hit a dead end. I knew I was in the right place, but the map showed nothing specific to indicate where the treasure was hidden. Maybe the bell was made of solid silver or gold. Flipping open my pocketknife, I reached up and notched the edge. Nope! The metal was the muted color of brass.

With my mind racing a million miles an hour, I thought about the infinity symbol I had seen down on the boat. Perhaps this was a similar situation, and I'd find some sort of symbol or marking that would direct me to the treasure. Maybe I was supposed to look for a trap door or some kind of secret compartment. Spinning around, I scanned my surroundings but saw nothing of the kind. Perhaps I should have been looking for another metaphor, but the map had indicated that this was the spot. I was just missing it! Without warning, the massive bronze bell swung out and nearly knocked me over the edge. It was five o'clock! My game was about to start.

CLANG!

My head felt like it was going to explode from the ear-shattering sounds of the bell. Sinking to my knees, I felt like a jewel thief who'd accidentally triggered a jewelry store alarm. The bell was going to alert everyone to my position. I would be caught red-handed.

CLANG!

Nothing like a runaway imagination to get your heart going! Nobody knew where I was, so I quickly put a stop to the fear of being caught and concentrated on protecting my ears. The sound coming from the striking bell was deafening, and I still had to wait out three more strikes!

CLANG!

I looked up to find the source of the piercing clangor, and the swinging bell missed my face by inches, if not centimeters. I closed my eyes and put my head between my knees, which gave me an up-close and personal whiff of the pigeon poop wafting up from my Wallabees.

CLANG!

With my eyes closed, I noticed that the bell tower was rocking back and forth, a result of the swinging motion of the large bell. It was more than large—it was huge and it probably weighed as much as a Volkswagen Bug. Okay, that was probably an exaggeration, but the way the tower shook back and forth, I knew the bell had to weigh a lot.

CLANG!

As the final strike of the bell marked the end of the blaring assault on my eardrums, I slowly opened my eyes. Gathering my thoughts, which had been scattered by the ear-splitting clangor, I was blinded by the reflection of the sun bouncing off the face of my wristwatch.

Turning my head to the side, my eyes followed the reflection to a crack in the overhead plaster of the bell tower. As I turned my wrist, I noticed a glistening light shining back at me like a lighthouse beacon.

I dug into my backpack, grabbed my flashlight, flicked it on and stood on my tiptoes for a closer look. It was no use. From where I was standing, I couldn't see anything, so I hoisted myself up and onto the ledge of the bell tower. When I directed the beam of my flashlight into the crack in the plaster, the glistening intensified. My heart raced. Using the butt-end of my flashlight, I chipped away some of the plaster. Suddenly, a silver Piece of Eight fell into my palm. At that moment, I realized that the entire canopy of the bell tower was filled with gold and silver coins. I had found the lost treasure of Jean Lafitte!

TREASURE TIP

The worst defeat is the defeat that occurs inside the mind.

33

A GAME TO REMEMBER

D itching my bike at the bike racks, I caught sight
of my mom and dad in the stands. Dad immediately called out to me, wanting to know why
I was still dressed in my street clothes, but I had no time to
explain. I simply waved back to him and ducked into the
dugout.

"I told you not to be late," Gary said, stuffing my uniform
in my arms.

"Yeah, yeah, I know. But I need to tell you something,"
I whispered.

"Scott!" Coach Palmer shouted, rushing over, clutching the starting line-up. "Get dressed. Game's about to start."

"I need to talk to my brother first."

"No time for chitchat, son. Time's a wastin'," Coach Palmer said, ushering me out of the dugout.

As I crossed to the bathrooms by the snack bar, I looked to see if Jaq was sitting with my parents, but she wasn't. Where was she? She was never one to miss our games. I could not believe it. I had the biggest secret in the history of secrets and nobody to share it with.

Finally, I saw a familiar face. Jimmy was near the bleachers listening to his dad's last-minute words of advice. Rushing over, excited to reveal what I had discovered, I heard Jimmy tell his dad this would be his last baseball game. He said he wanted to get involved with the state science fair competition next year and he didn't love playing baseball anymore. When Sheriff Finn questioned his son's declaration, Jimmy said something I'll never forget.

"Dad, I'm not you, and I'm not my big brother. I'm okay at sports, and while this is fun, I don't want to be a professional baseball player. I want to do what I want to do."

Sheriff Finn smiled at Jimmy and put his arm around him. "Son, you're right. I'll support you in whatever you want to do. If you want to be an astronaut, I'm there for you."

"Let's not get crazy, Dad," Jimmy said with a laugh. "I'm just saying I want to see how things work out. I like math, and I'm really good at it."

Standing up to his dad had to be hard for Jimmy to do, but then something occurred to me. It was hard for the *old* Jimmy. The pudgy kid walking towards me was a *new* Jimmy altogether. Even his step displayed a new lease on life. He seemed happier. He seemed more confident than ever before. He was different. Come to think of it, we all were, and I didn't want to take away from Jimmy's self-defining moment by telling him about the treasure. Not yet, anyway.

I guess the time wasn't right to tell anyone about the treasure, which is why I turned and headed to the bathrooms to change into my uniform. When I reached the door, I ran right into Tommy Osborne, who was exiting.

"Watch where you're going, Geek!" Tommy said.

"Tommy. Hey, how's it going?" I said with a smile.

"Ready to strike out again, Shorty?" he said in his normal venomous tone. "Wearing your backpack to the game? What a dork. You guys are going down!"

I simply extended my hand. "May the best man win."

The gesture threw him off balance for more than a second. I'm sure he was expecting some type of sarcasm from me, which was the norm for our relationship, but I continued to hold out my hand.

"I'm gonna strike you out," he said, refusing to shake my hand.

"Good luck with that," I replied.

"Tommy!" A booming voice suddenly ripped into our conversation. It was Coach Osborne, and he was not pleased to say the least. "Get your butt in the dugout. Now!"

Tommy lowered his head and walked past his old man, keeping himself out of arm's length. As he passed Coach Osborne, he looked back at me, trying to figure me out. He had no clue that I was different and the world before me was different too.

Much like our previous game, the first few innings rushed past without incident. The score was knotted at 0–0, and we were in another pitcher's duel. Zippy was throwing better than he had ever thrown before. So far, he had more strikeouts than Tommy. When I saw Coach Osborne pacing in front of his team's dugout like a caged dog at the city animal shelter, I knew the statistic was not sitting well with him. The man was not accustomed to the prospect of losing a championship, especially to a ragtag team of misfits like us.

As fate would have it, we entered the bottom of the ninth with the score still tied at 0-0 and one out. I felt as if life was giving me another opportunity to succeed when Tommy threw a wild pitch. The errant throw caught Zippy's shoulder and he was awarded first base.

Stepping into the batter's box, I remembered the last game when I had struck out. I also remembered what Old Man Sheesley had said about swinging for the fences. By swinging for the fences, I was only defeating myself. If I had learned one thing today, it was never to cause my own defeat ever again.

This was one of those moments in life when we say, "Why does this keep happening to me?" Then I realized that moments like this happened so I could learn the lesson. The sooner I learned the lesson, the sooner this experience would stop happening over and over again. Well, it sounded like good advice, but I knew I still needed to swing the bat to make contact. I felt uneasy, but stepped forward nonetheless, searching for my confidence.

I looked into the stands and saw Mom and Dad cheering from their usual spots, but still no sign of Jaq. How could she miss the most important game of the season? Scanning the bleachers for her, I saw Brandy Larson sitting in the front row with her clique of popular girlfriends. They were whispering to each other, and the girl with the red hair directed Brandy's attention to me. She looked up and smiled. What? Wait a second. Did I just see Brandy Larson smile at me? Confused, I looked behind me to see if she was smiling at Tommy, but she was not. She was smiling at me. My heart began to pound. Then, still looking at me, she started to say something.

"Let's go! You can do it!" she yelled. "Strike this sucker out, Tommy."

A flood of anger rushed through me like never before. Forget the base hit. Now I wanted to hit the cover off the ball and show this girl a thing or two. I stepped back into the batter's box and dug my left foot into the moistened dirt of home plate, followed by my right foot. I was fired up and ready to cream the ball into smithereens.

"Looks like it's time for another strike out, eh Shorty?" the catcher snapped up at me.

Now my blood was boiling. Before I knew what was happening, Tommy fired a laser at me. My bat froze in position and never left my shoulder.

"*Steeeeerike* one!" the umpire yelled.

"Come on, Scooter!" Zippy yelled from first base, standing next to one of the Amato twins.

Joe laughed. "Yeah, come on, Scooter! Swing for the fences and strike out the way you always do."

"Don't listen to him, Baby Bro. Put a good swing on it!" Gary called from behind me.

Baby Bro? I was not a baby! With a tangled web of thoughts powering through my head, I saw the next pitch leave Tommy's hand in a flash. It was another fastball drifting high. I swung with all my might.

"*Steeeeerike* two!" the umpire yelled again.

It was as if everything in me had turned into stone. I watched what was happening as if from the stands as a spectator. I was allowing the situation and my anger to dictate my actions. I was listening to my ego, wanting to

hit the cover off the baseball. I had forgotten the agreement
I'd made with myself during the long hike down from the
cave. Before Tommy could throw another pitch, I stepped
out of the batter's box to regroup.

"Stay off the high stuff, man!" Zippy yelled.

"Level swing, son!" my dad offered.

"Strike him out, Tommy!" Brandy added.

I knew I had to calm down, so I took in a long, deep
breath. I shut out all the sounds around me and let go of
any thought I had of failure. In essence, I focused on my
beating heart and became still. I recalled what I had learned
today. I remembered that getting angry would only block
my talents. I knew I could hit Tommy's pitch out of the
park, but right now my team needed a base hit. A base
hit was just as good as a home run, and it was high time I
learned this lesson.

As I scanned my surroundings, I felt as if I was in a silent
movie—those eight-millimeter movies my grandparents
watched when they were kids. I was energized with a
confidence I'd only dreamed of. I had made the decision
simply to make contact with the ball and let the chips fall
where they would fall.

Stepping back into the batter's box, I felt a calmness warm
over me. The adrenalin rush from trying to hit the cover off
the ball had subsided. Each breath I took was deeper than
the one before, and the process finally caused my heartbeat
to slow down to its normal tempo. I was almost relaxed. I
felt so good that when I looked up at Tommy, I think I even
smiled at him. I could tell that this made him furious, but I
did not care. I felt good, and that was all that mattered.

As Tommy moved into his wind-up, I released any
residual fear of striking out. *Base hit ... Line drive ... Base hit
... Line drive,* I repeated like a mantra.

It was like I was watching the pitch leave Tommy's hand in slow motion. I was watching the ball better than ever before. I could see the red laces spinning towards me in a perfect circle. This meant the pitch was not a curve ball, because when a curve ball is thrown, the laces spin from side to side, dropping the trajectory of the ball to the side it was spinning towards. This was his best pitch. This was his red-hot fastball, and I saw it coming as clear as the morning sunrise on a summer day. But something different was happening. The pitch was rising up into the high fastball. I did not panic. I simply lifted the bat from my shoulder and swung, nice and easy.

34

MAKING CONTACT

I felt like Reggie Jackson, the way my arms extended towards the bottom of my swing. It was picture perfect. My chin was tucked into my chest, and my eyes were locked on the baseball. I think it was the first time in my short baseball career that I actually heard the crack of the bat as my trusty wooden Louisville Slugger made contact with the ball.

CRACK!

The ball jumped from my bat like a super ball bouncing on the sidewalk. The sounds of the game, the cheering of the crowd and the voice of Coach Osborne screaming at his players to move back all returned as if I'd bolted awake from a dream. I took off running towards first base. Imagining the black bear running after us on Woodbury Island, I started to run faster than I had ever run before. All I needed to do was reach first base and stay out of a double play. Gary was on deck. He could hit us in. I finally understood the concept of team play: rely on others to achieve the desired goal.

From the reaction of the cheering crowd, I knew it had to be a base hit, but I still kept my focus on the bag at first base. Then I looked up and saw the ball drifting high in the air. It was a high fly ball, and Chris Amato was running back towards the fence in left field. My heart sank and skipped a beat because Chris Amato was the fastest kid on their team, even faster than his brother, who was as fast as a cheetah. I knew he was going to catch the first ball I had ever hit off of Tommy, and I was going to be called out. I could hear the guys rubbing it in: *We told you to lay off the high fastball.*

I lowered my eyes and began to slow my run. Then I heard the crowd roar. Chris Amato must have had made a brilliant running catch. When the roar grew even louder, I looked up to see him merely standing in left field, watching the ball sail over the fence. I had done it. I had hit a home run!

As I rounded the bases, I saw my teammates running from the dugout. Ball caps and gloves were flying in the air as they rushed towards home plate. Rounding second, I began the home run trot made famous by Mr. October himself, Reggie Jackson. It was hard to believe that I had just hit a home run, because it felt like I had barely swung the bat. All I had done was swing smoothly, keeping my eyes focused on the ball, and nothing else.

Even though I hated him for what he had done to us, Old Man Sheesley was right: *The harder you try, the harder it gets.* The secret is to relax, take a deep breath and let it flow!

We met the Crab Shack Cardinals in the middle of the field to show good sportsmanship, which was required by all teams of Jefferson County Little League. This was something I had never looked forward to, because before today, I was known as the "Strikeout King," even when we did manage to win. I knew what it was like to lose, so I did not gloat when we slapped the hands of the losers. We slapped hands with the Amato Twins, little Danny Simon, and even Harrison Tweed. I could only imagine how much he must have wanted to be on our team right about then, but he was not. Those buck teeth would have to find their own way to smile, because this victory was ours, and we were not about to share it with a traitor. When I reach Tommy, the last in the line of all the Crab Shack Cardinal players, he did not slap my hand. He simply reached out for a handshake. I shook his hand and smiled.

"Feel lucky?" he asked.

"It's the luckiest day of my life," I said, thinking about the gold and silver coins in the canopy of the bell tower.

He looked at me oddly and congratulated me before saying, "I'm going to strike you out the next time you step into that batter's box."

"I look forward to the challenge," I said with a smile.

We continued to celebrate on our way back to the dugout, where we stopped and shouted the game-ending chant:

Two! Four! Six! Eight!
Who do we appreciate!
Crab Shack Cardinals! Yeah!

Before the chant ended, I was mobbed into a massive dog pile celebration. Though I could barely breathe with everyone on top of me, giving me noogies in the arm and head, it was worth it. The entire day had been worth every moment.

When we moved the celebration to the stands so we could share the excitement with our family and friends, I noticed a girl standing on the outskirts of the crowd. She was staring directly at me. When my line of sight finally cleared, which was a matter of pure luck with the mob of congratulations surrounding me, I finally recognized her. The girl was Jaq. She was wearing a jeans skirt and flower-print blouse. I couldn't have imagined her dressing up, but with her hair down, shining and combed back perfectly, I had to admit, she looked beautiful. That must be why I had not recognized her at first. It was the most amazing transformation I had ever seen. I'm not sure what kind of look I had on my face, but I felt a huge smile warming through me. I could tell she was embarrassed because of the way her hand twisted the edge of her blouse.

I could hardly believe this was the girl I had spent the entire day with on Woodbury Island. I could not believe this was the girl who could throw a baseball better than any of us. Without missing a beat, I cut through the crowd to meet her. But just as I was about to reach her, Brandy Larson stepped in front of me.

"Hey, Scooter," she said, smiling wide.

The greeting shook me a bit because I was not sure she even knew my name, let alone my nickname.

"Hi … um … Brandy," I said nervously.

"I had no idea you could hit the baseball like that."

I did not say anything. I just looked past her and saw disappointment crossing Jaq's face. Brandy turned and noticed Jaq standing behind her.

"Wow! Jaq? Is that you? I barely recognized you. Nice skirt," Brandy said, rolling her eyes as she turned to face me again. "So, Scott, are you going to the fireworks show tonight?"

"What?" I asked, confused by the sudden attention

"The fireworks show. The Fourth of July picnic," Brandy said, flipping her hair. The girl did have great hair. Everyone knew that. "Anyway, maybe I'll see you there, watching the fireworks."

When I looked past Brandy again, I saw Jaq turning to walk away.

"Brandy? Would you excuse me?" I said as I brushed past her to stop Jaq's retreat.

"Hi," I said softly. "Is she still standing behind me?"

Jaq answered me with a nod. "You should go with her. It's fine, really," she said quietly. "That's what you've been waiting for, isn't it?"

"Brandy?" I said, turning around and addressing the girl of my dreams.

"Yes?" she said with the corners of her mouth rising into a smile.

"I'm sorry, but I already have plans to watch the fireworks."

"With who? The tomboy?" Brandy said with a laugh.

"Tomboy? Where? I don't see a tomboy," I said, turning back to Jaq. "I just see the most beautiful girl in the whole wide world."

Jaq smiled through the tears that welled up in her eyes.

"Loser!" Brandy said stomping away. "I'd never go with you anyway."

Jaq and I stood there for a second before she could finally say anything.

"Really?"

"Really," I answered, as we started walking back towards the others.

"No. Wait," she said, giving in to the insecurity that was visibly flowing through her. "I look stupid. I want to go home and change. You go ahead."

"Jaq, trust me. You look amazing."

Before she had a chance to believe any of the runaway thoughts in her mind, I took her hand and started back towards the others.

I glanced to the side and noticed Old Man Sheesley standing nearby, watching us. He looked different. His beard was trimmed and he looked clean. I wondered what could have made the old man clean himself up, because I barely recognized him. Even though he had tried to kill us, I felt like we were kindred spirits in some strange way, and I felt sorry for him. I had no idea what it was like to be alone in life. I had a great group of friends and an amazing family. Old Man Sheesley was alone.

"Give me a second," I said, turning to Jaq before crossing over to Old Man Sheesley.

"Nice hit," he said in his gruff voice. "Works wonders when you don't try so hard, doesn't it?"

"Guess it does. Looks like you made it back okay. I like the new beard."

"I have you guys to thank for that. That darn saltwater taffy is some sticky stuff," he said, finding a smile. "Your Mom's, I take it?"

"Only the best."

"I'm sorry that I had to lie to you guys at my house the other night."

"Let's not forget about trying to bury us alive in the cave!"

"Well, I knew you'd be okay," he said with a shrug of the shoulders.

"Really? Is that what you were thinking when you dislodged the railroad tie?"

"Is that what you were thinking when you guys hit me with that bomb?"

"A saltwater taffy bomb is a little different than trapping someone inside a cave, don't you think?"

"All's fair in the hunt for treasure, I guess." Old Man Sheesley replied.

"I guess," I answered as the moment passed between us like two warriors registering mutual respect.

I thought that was pretty cool, to be treated like an equal by an adult. Who knew? Maybe this would be the start of a friendship.

"But I meant what I said," Old Man Sheesley added, "about being happy and what matters most in life."

"Yeah, thanks for that. I had a lot of time to think about stuff walking back to the harbor. But there's one thing I don't understand."

"What's that?" Old Man Sheesley leaned forward.

"If you know all that stuff about life and what matters most, why don't you live it?"

"What do you mean?"

Looking past him, I directed his attention to Ms. Benson selling baked goods at the library's fundraising table.

"Someday, I guess," he replied.

"You waiting until you get a bit older?" I said with a chuckle. "Don't you think it's time you start living your life—today?"

Old Man Sheesley nodded and offered me slight smile. "Life is good ... but I suppose it could always get better," he said as he extended his hand in friendship. "So I guess you discovered the map was worthless?"

"Well, I wouldn't say that, old man."

"Wait a minute!" His eyes grew wide. "You solved it?"

"Let's just say the treasure is around us every day, letting us know—as you said—that life is always good."

I smiled and walked back to Jaq, who was now surrounded by Zippy, Jimmy and Gary. They too were fascinated by Jaq's transformation, but Jimmy had a strange look on his face.

"What's wrong?" I asked.

"Zip?" Gary said. "Tell him."

"Fatman's gone," Zippy said softly.

"What do you mean, gone? What about our free sundaes?"

"See? That's what I said," Jimmy added.

"Fatman's on vacation," Zippy continued.

"I still don't believe it," Jimmy said as the thought of no ice cream sank into his sweets-obsessed mind. "Fatman's never left town. Why now, all of a sudden? I think we should go and check, just to make sure."

"Jimmy, give it up. My mom said she saw him hanging up the sign when she was on her way to the game. He's on vacation," Zippy repeated.

"I say good for him," Jaq said, joining in. "He's finally getting out of this place for a while."

"I bet you he went to see the Jackson 5 concert in Seattle." I guessed.

"That would be rad," Zippy said.

"Least he could've left us the keys to watch over things," Jimmy said, bummed that there would be no free ice cream, which always tasted better than when you had to pay for it.

"So you could eat all his ice cream?" Zippy added. "Fatman knows better than that."

As the others carried on the normal chitchat about ice cream, I looked over to see Old Man Sheesley buying some cookies from Ms. Benson's bake sale. He smiled my way and gave me the thumbs up as she turned around to count the change for his purchases. I looked past these two unsuspecting lovers to the bell tower of the Lafitte Public Library. It began to announce that it was seven o'clock. With each strike of the bell, my smile grew wider. Turning away from the bell tower, I interrupted my friends' conversation about lighting sparklers and eating barbecue before the big fireworks show.

"You guys want to go see something really cool?"

"And miss out on the barbecue?" Jimmy said, smacking his lips as if he could already taste the hickory sauce of his dad's barbecued chicken.

"I'm with Jimmy on this one, Scooter," Zippy said. "I'm starving."

"Me, too," Gary chimed in. "Been kind of a long day."

"But worth every second," Jimmy said, smiling at everyone.

"Trust me, guys. You're gonna want to see this," I said, trying to convince them without just blurting out the location of the treasure.

I wanted them to feel the rush of excitement that would come when they saw the gold and silver in the bell tower. They had worked too hard simply to be told where the treasure was. This was something they needed to experience firsthand.

When my attempts to convince them failed, I finally gave up, and that was okay. The treasure had been hidden for over forty years. One more day would not hurt. Then I noticed that I was feeling something different again. It was like everything was cool. I was in a place where I did not want anything other than the joy of friendship and the celebration of the Fourth of July. I was not even wishing for a new bike, and for me that was a big deal.

Then I began to wonder why. Was it because I had seen the lost treasure of Jean Lafitte? Was it because I had just hit a home run? Was it because I had found out how much I cared about Jaq? I did not know, but I did know that I was happy. From where I stood and with who I was, I was indeed happy. I was not thinking about the lost treasure of Jean Lafitte at all. Well, okay, maybe just a little, but my friends were more important, and I wanted to eat barbecue, light sparklers and maybe hold Jaq's hand during the fireworks show.

"You okay?" Jaq said, arriving next to me as I stared up at the bell tower.

"Oh yeah. Life is good," I said with a smile.

Jaq took my hand, and we joined the others at the bike racks. Climbing onto our bikes, we all smiled at each other as the sound of Chicago's "Saturday in the Park" rang out from a group of teenagers gathered around a new convertible Camero. In a few short years, we would probably be standing around one of our own cars listening to music, but right now we were happy with our bikes. Being thirteen years old was not so bad. I would be older soon enough, so I was happy to live this moment with everything I had.

Today was a great day. In fact, this had been the best summer of our lives—one we would never forget. It was a time of adventure, baseball and saltwater taffy. And love, of course. Because in the end, that's what life is really about. Love.

THE END

A FINAL WORD

Have you ever worried about something so long that it makes you sick to your stomach? Has a thought ever made you feel dizzy? It's taken me almost four decades to understand that *energy flows where attention goes*. If you think about something long enough, sooner or later, good or bad, it's going to affect your life.

If we know this to be true, why not let go of any thought that makes us feel uneasy? If you're going to spend your time and energy on a thought, why not unleash thoughts that make you happy? Why not focus on something that might help you get what you want out of life? If you've answered yes to any of my questions, then I'll ask you one more: Are you willing to do whatever it takes?

I ask this question of you because here's the thing about life and getting what you want out of it: Your happiness is up to you. Not your parents. Not your teachers. Not your friends. Not even your brother or your sister. Sure, these people are important in your life—but your life is YOUR life. Everything in your life starts and ends with you.

So, where do you start? You start by following your heart. Whatever makes you happy in life is the direction you need to follow. Your heart is like a compass, constantly guiding you through life. When you feel like you can't find your way, it's because you have lost a connection to your heart. Your heart keeps you on course, like the treasure map in our story. When you have a relationship with your heart, you never, ever, ever have to feel as if you're alone. Your heart is always with you. This is why I refer to it as your compass. Listen to your heart. Follow your dreams and never look back.

How do you get there? You get there by losing the fear of the unknown. You will never know what you love until you give it a try. Your life is yours to explore from this day forward. The sooner you find out what makes you happy, the sooner you will begin to experience it on a regular basis.

Have you ever asked yourself the question, "What makes me happy?" If you haven't, now is a perfect time to start. Ask yourself, "What makes me happy?" In fact, ask yourself the question out loud. I say this because when you ask it out loud, you hear it and become involved with the desire to find the answer. When you do that, you set yourself on the adventure, and that's what life is about— discovering what you love. Your life is an adventure.

"Playing video games" or "hanging out with my friends" isn't the answer you're looking for to the question,

"What makes me happy?" What we're talking about here is learning that happiness isn't something you "get"—it's something you "bring" to everything you do! Wherever you go, happiness is there because you are there.

There's nothing wrong with playing video games or hanging out with your friends, but if it merely provides you with distraction so you can avoid boredom, how good can it actually be? Once you finish school, your life will be consumed with your day job. Wouldn't it be cool to think of that day job as something you love to do? If you love it, you'll never have to work a day in your life. If you love animals, perhaps your life adventure is to become a veterinarian. If you love to swim, maybe your life adventure is to become a rescue swimmer with the Coast Guard. If you love clothes, maybe your life adventure will be as a clothing designer.

You might think that you are too young to start thinking about your day job, but you aren't. Trust me. I know. Time is of the essence. Do not delay! Life moves faster than you think, so the sooner you decide on your adventure, the sooner you'll get to experience more happiness in your life. You'll experience more happiness because you are doing what you love. You'll love who you are. Sounds easy enough, doesn't it?

By starting your adventure today, you are willing to lose the dis-ability of living your life on a conditional basis. What do I mean by conditional? "When I get older, I'm going to be happy. When I meet the right girl or boy, yes, then I'll be happy." When you do this, you put conditions on your happiness. You are delaying your happiness for some time other than right now. The past is history and the future is unwritten, but right now is happening—right now!

You have a choice to be happy or angry the moment you get out of bed. Everything is a choice. Trust me when

I say that choosing happiness is a lot more fun. Choosing happiness is an adventure. Choosing anger is a nightmare.

When you make an agreement with yourself that no person and no thing can divert you from being happy, your life will begin to lift off and you will soar with adventure in everything you do. Sounds silly, but isn't it cool to think of doing what you love for the rest of your life? Isn't it cool to think that you are different from everyone else? You are special. Treat yourself that way and never worry about what other people think of you. You are you, so be the best you possible!

Sure, life can be hard, especially at your age. Right now you are trying to figure out who you are and where you belong. This can be confusing, I know, but trust me when I tell you that you belong in the company of happiness. Nothing else is worthwhile. When your soul (your heart compass) is connected to what you love, and you love who you are, love is what you'll get in return. If, on the other hand, you practice being angry or afraid, that's what you'll get. Don't be afraid. Be bold. Live each moment in sync with your heart and you will always be protected.

Making decisions is just listening to what your heart tells you and then doing it—fearlessly and filled with passion— No matter what!

When you finally decide on something—and that's the big thing: making a decision—you've got to go after it. The thing that makes you happy will be your gift to the rest of us. Imagine if Picasso had ignored his heart compass. Our museums wouldn't be filled with his work, which we appreciate so much. What about Mark Twain? Imagine if he had not written about Tom Sawyer and he simply tried to fit in so he could be part of the crowd. We would not be able to experience his gift of literature.

Don't worry that you might make a wrong decision. Nothing you go through is wrong if it brings you closer to what you love doing. I was once fired from a job, and while it was a bummer at the time, I later discovered that I had to lose that job to find the job I'm in now. Nothing just happens in life. Everything happens for a reason, as Old Man Sheesley reminded us.

You will probably change your mind a million times before you get to be my age, and that is perfectly okay. I did that. But you must choose an adventure and go for it— always making sure you are in love with your decision. At the end of the day, all you need is love. Once you experience love, the adventure of this life only gets better. Now find it. See it. Be it.

LOVE

If you are interested in finding out how to live each day, each moment, from a happier, more joy-filled place called love, please visit www.SaltwaterTaffyBook.com to download *Another Piece of Saltwater Taffy—A Toolbox for Getting What You Want.*

Always remember that you are special. Always remember that you are different from everyone else, and that's what makes you special. You are lacking nothing.

YOU ARE ... LOVE.

ALWAYS REMEMBER ...
EVERY MOMENT IS ANOTHER ADVENTURE
WAITING TO HAPPEN.

—Eric "Uncle E" DelaBarre
Author, *Saltwater Taffy*

ABOUT THE AUTHOR

ERIC DELABARRE is an award-winning filmmaker and speaker and, most recently, the ghostwriter of a best-selling title for *Random House/Harmony Books*. Eric began his career with Universal Studios on NBC's mega-hit drama, *Law & Order*. His work has been sold around the world and showcased on HBO, Cinemax, Showtime, Starz/Encore, USA Network and NBC. He is the author of *Why Not; Start Living Your Life Today* and past-president of the *Boys & Girls Club of Santa Monica Council*. He lives and works in Santa Monica, California, with his wife, Julie, and is an avid mountain biker.

ABOUT THE ILLUSTRATOR

R. C. NASON, a professional artist for more than twenty years, is a recipient of the Hans Christian Anderson Award for *Thumbelina*. With extensive film credits for illustrating and painting for animated feature films, Rob specializes in translating a story line into exciting visuals. He has work with companies such as 20th Century Fox, Harper Collins, Hallmark and Sony, to name but a few. When away from his studio, he is sketching in the field for discovery, usually in the Lakes Region of New Hampshire or northern Ontario. Canadian by birth, Rob currently lives in the United States with his wife, Nancy, and shares each adventure of his life with his two boys, Nick and Cody.

ATTENTION TAFFY HEADS!

On the pages of this book,
a hidden treasure awaits.

SOLVE THE CIPHER!
FIND THE TREASURE!

For more information visit
www.SaltwaterTaffyBook.com
and sign up for the

SALTWATER TAFFY TREASURE HUNT

Who knows?
You could be the TAFFY HEAD to win the

SALTWATER TAFFY
GRAND PRIZE!